LOVE LIKE WATER

Hearts in Hendricks Book One

D.E. MALONE

LOVE LIKE WATER

Cover designed by Seedlings Design Studio

First Edition

Summary: After losing her job as an inn manager, Darcy Conti goes to work for a local tour company and ends up falling for her boss's son, the man she was hired to replace.

Life-sustaining,
Ever-changing,
Raging river,
Drops aquiver,
An earthly calm,
And heart's true balm,
Like Love,
Like Water.

- Silas Penn

Chapter One

⁂

Labor Day weekend hadn't been nearly long enough to suit Sean Stetman.

His cabin near Three Forks was still bare-bones empty, but to him it was the perfect refuge. The fishing had been terrific. The quiet was ideal. If it were up to him, he'd move up there tomorrow and go off grid. But Emily, his mother, quashed that idea before it had fully formed. Thanks to his younger brother, Matt, and his big mouth, Sean's wish for a permanent escape was not conducive to running the family business. His conversation with Matt over the weekend was more wishful thinking aloud than a solid plan. Sooner or later there would be payback for Matt's indiscretion.

As mothers do, Emily must have tuned into the negative vibes flowing from his office and into the front lobby of Sturgeon Widows Tours. She poked her head into the room, a space not much larger than a closet.

"Are you ready? The guests are outside."

Sean recrossed his ankles, which he'd propped up on his desk. "In a minute."

"You really should show your face, even if you're not the main attraction anymore." Emily studied her son's expression until he turned to flick the switch off on his mini coffeemaker. Sean poured fresh coffee into his insulated mug, prompting Emily to let out an exaggerated sigh. "I thought I'd be doing you a favor by letting you step back from guiding. Are you going to give me a hard time about driving too?"

He screwed the lid back on and brought the cup to his lips, taking a long, equally exaggerated sip while he kept his eyes on her. Finally, he brought the cup away from his mouth. "No."

Emily pressed her lips together in a tight smile. "Good." She snapped her fingers. "And I've got a lead on a new guide." She lowered her voice. "Melina is NOT the person to take over for you." She looked over her shoulder and out the front window to the tour guests gathered on the balcony, enjoying a pretour breakfast where Melina Pereja, the company's business manager, sat amidst the good-sized group, trying to keep up with the small talk. She was failing miserably by the look on her face.

"Good, because we're probably losing references. No one in their right mind would recommend us after listening to her drone on and on for three hours." Over Emily's shoulder, Sean saw Melina glancing toward the lobby as if she needed rescuing.

Emily handed him the tour manifest. "But she's

fantastically organized. That's worth more to me now than a gift for small talk. And she's very pretty."

"How does that qualify her to work here?" he asked flatly.

"It doesn't," Emily replied. "Not at all."

His mother's poorly suppressed smile didn't escape Sean's notice, but he pretended he didn't see it. He read over the guest list for the morning. Twenty-two people. Almost to capacity.

He understood why Emily hired her. Melina couldn't pretend she liked socializing with their guests, but she had mastered the behind-the-scenes logistics of tour planning and taking care of the books. Still, working for Sturgeon Widows Tours, a person had to be flexible, a multitasker. Melina had proved herself not to be that person after Emily first asked her to cover a tour for Sean. A few negative reviews rolled in during the weeks following the tours that Melina led. Sean guessed, too, that his mother had an ulterior motive. He'd heard enough of Emily's casual remarks about Melina since she was hired at the beginning of the summer. "She's very smart. And funny too!" Emily reminded him every so often. Or she'd try to appeal to his outdoor interests, by mentioning her family has vacationed in Two Rivers ever since she was a baby. "They own a cabin there," she offered. But when Emily realized that her coyness couldn't convince Sean to ask her out, Emily would resort to the direct approach, saying, "You can't deny she's very pretty," like Emily had just repeated for the umpteenth time. Yes, Sean understood his mom's motive. It was another reason why he longed to escape to the cabin. Alone.

He brushed past his mom, setting his mug down on the counter, to pull his denim jacket off the hook by the front door. "After I'm finished with this group, I'm heading out."

"You are not putting in another half day. There's too much to do."

He stopped. "I didn't say I was taking the day off after the tour, did I?"

Emily was silent.

"I scheduled an appointment for new brakes on Clyde, remember?"

His mother looked at the ceiling because of the names he'd given to the company's two buses—Clyde and Clem. She'd even referred to them by name a time or two. "Fine." Then she softened, her shoulders slumping. "I'm sorry I forgot."

"Always so quick to blame." He forced a smile. "I'm not that much of a slacker."

"I didn't call you a slacker. It's just with Matt starting his new job in town and you...taking on a different position."

Sean juggled the keys in his hand. "We've talked about going bigger for years—hiring more people, developing more tours, moving. Maybe now is the time to look into that more seriously."

His mother sighed heavily. "That's an even bigger task than finding a new tour guide." She waved her hand. "That's a conversation for another time. I haven't yet gotten used to shifting around the responsibilities."

A twinge of guilt touched Sean, and he looked toward the group on the balcony. "Maybe this will be temporary. Maybe I'll want my old job back."

"Don't worry about it. We'll manage. What's important is that you get your head on straight again."

Sean nodded. Yes. Even he realized that wanting to hide out in his cabin for the rest of his life would be pretty bizarre behavior. Yet it was completely justified given the circumstances of the last nine months.

Outside, Sean approached the group, and he almost cringed at his effect on them. Coffee cups hovered midair. Conversation paused. Men noticed their wives' prolonged stares. Genetics had gifted him with his mother's dark, striking features and his father's unassuming nature. He often caught strangers staring and wondered if part of his breakfast dangled from his beard or if he'd skipped a shirt button. Sometimes he resented the attention.

"Good morning, sunshine," Melina said, patting the empty seat next to her. "We're just finishing up." She gathered her hair behind her neck with both hands and pulled it out of her jacket collar. Her hair fell in waves halfway down her back, which didn't escape Sean's attention. If he was anywhere near being in a dating mindset, he would have asked Melina out to dinner or a movie when he'd first met her. Sadly, once he got to know her, he realized she was far from his type, even though his mother thought otherwise.

Sean waved off her invitation. "No, thanks. I'll be sitting for the next few hours."

He looked away when her smile faltered and busied himself with greeting the guests. They were mostly older couples this morning, except for a family of four with two teen girls. He pulled the phone out of his back pocket to look at the time when the mother asked how soon they'd be leaving. She needed a coffee refill.

"No need to rush," he assured her. "We have a good ten minutes before we need to be on the road."

Sean glanced back at Melina. He'd been harsh with her a moment ago, but her constant angling to get close to him annoyed the heck out of him. An apology crossed his mind, but then she shuffled the papers in her lap, and her lips started moving as she silently read the tour script, and the idea passed. Melina was a recent University of Minnesota-Duluth graduate who had two things on her mind: moving to a bigger city as soon as possible and bringing Sean with her. Ever since Melina joined the company, Sean spent most of his time thinking up creative excuses on why he couldn't take her out. The woman was unable to take a hint and, as if on cue, Melina closed the binder and left her seat to stand next to him.

"Your mom can't hire someone fast enough for this job. I'm exhausted being 'on' for hours during these tours," she said behind her hand. "How do you do it?"

Sean glanced sideways at her and stifled a biting comment about caring about their customers, who deserved their money's worth in a quality tour. He considered pointing out she could stand to learn a little more about Hendricks—about the lake, trails, and streams, its history, and the people who called this place home—to begin with. To Melina, Hendricks was a stopping point on the way to bigger ambitions. He knew the type well.

"It can be tiring," he said instead, opting to not start the day on a negative note. "But it's easier if you love your subject."

Melina's eyebrows pinched together at the subtle dig, but she rebounded with her ready-made smile. "That's why you're so good at it." She leaned against his arm and lowered her voice. "I can really tell how much you love this place. And who wouldn't? Duluth doesn't have the same vibe as the small towns up here."

Sean almost laughed aloud. Knowing her preference for big cities, Sean wondered how she planned to seduce him away from his Hendricks roots. If his mother wasn't paying Melina a generous salary with the hope she'd be the one to get his head straightened out, Melina would have been back to her big city dreams by now.

"No, it definitely suits me just fine. Always has, always will."

Melina opened up the leather-bound file for the tour notes, studying them. "You know, I wonder if some of these tour stops could be updated a bit?"

"Oh?" Sean waited for her to continue.

She let out a breathy laugh. "I mean, aren't our guests almost all women? Hence, 'Sturgeon Widows Tours.' Maybe we should revamp the stops. Get rid of the Sage River and Red's Tavern stops."

"The Sturgeon Widows name is a historical term from Hendricks's past. We're not serving widows." Sean couldn't believe what he was hearing, but he wanted to know the rest. "Go on."

Encouraged, Melina tucked the book under her arm and

faced him. "I mean, the Sage River stop is all about the fishing industry history. Who wants to hear about that?"

Sean looked down at his feet while she talked because he wasn't sure he could keep his expression neutral.

"I get that the name 'Sturgeon Widows' came from the fishing industry, but do our clients really want to stop at a river? And just look at it?"

Sean chewed on his lip, still concentrating on his boots.

"And Red's Tavern? That's just a drink stop out on Highway 61. Couldn't we find a more upscale place in town to host it?" She tapped her finger against the book, thinking. "Maybe the Osage Tea Room? You know, the one near the pier? Maybe we should have lunch there, check the place out."

"I know where it is. I've been there," he said, and then instantly cursed himself for bringing it up.

Melina's eyes brightened. "Oh! With your mom?"

"No." He should have joined in a conversation with any one of these guests when he had the chance. His taciturn mood was taking a turn for the worse. He could tell she didn't like his answer because her smile wavered, though he really didn't care.

"You took someone else besides your mom to the tea room?" she teased. "Who was this lucky girl? Oh wait," she said, snapping her fingers. "The girlfriend. What was her name?...Payton...Pam..."

"Paige." His mother obviously had not been minding her own business since she was doing a pretty excellent job of sharing his with the world.

"That's right." Her face grew sympathetic. "I'm sorry. I shouldn't have pried."

"It's fine." He downed his coffee as he noticed the last of the tour guests tossing their empty breakfast plates onto the bus cart. "It looks like we're up."

Melina started as though she just then realized there were guests to tend to. She touched his arm again. "Listen, Sean. I'm sorry. Whatever happened between you and this Paige person is not my business."

He nodded. "Thanks," he said, and turned away toward the bus, gesturing over his shoulder to the guests who were congregating near the door that lead back into the lobby. "You'll need to remind them about bathrooms. We won't have a chance until nine thirty." He paused, his back still to her. "You know, at that drink stop. Red's Tavern."

Sean knew Melina's gaze bore into his back like a poison-tipped sword. He didn't usually take offense to most things, but Melina suggesting they change their tour itinerary was out of line. Those two stops had been on the program since the Stetmans opened their tour company twenty-four years ago. The Sage River stop off Highway 61 planted guests right at the mouth of the river where the seasonal salmon run emptied into Lake Superior. It was a beautiful stop with a small gravel parking lot and a short, even walk to a primitive shelter hewn from fallen birch logs. It was one of the most popular stops out of the twelve. He could count at least a half-dozen proposals taking place there over the years. Hell, even his dad had proposed to his mother there. But sentimentality aside, that stop was staying on the itinerary as long as there was a Sturgeon

Widows Tours company because it was relevant to the whole history of the Lake Superior fishing industry.

He climbed into the bus and turned the key in the ignition. Clem sputtered to life. He set his mug into the cupholder, glancing back toward Melina and the guests, who were making their way toward the bus. He took a deep breath and let it out slowly. The morning was cool enough that a barely visible vapor cloud hovered in front of his face for a moment. He took in the street in front of him, the green-and-black awnings on Higge Florist across the street, their neighbors since the beginning, and D & G Grocery, owned by his parents' close friends, Dave and Giselle Gladstone, on the opposite corner. The small boutique clothing and souvenir shops, artists' studios, coffee shops, and restaurants dotted both sides of Main Street for a half mile. The lake, in its ever-present glory, shone with a soft, tremulous light as the sun arced through the morning sky off to his left. He loved his hometown with a fierce protectiveness and resented that Melina didn't share the feeling. Should she even be working for a company that built its reputation on what Hendricks had to offer?

And if Melina wanted more details about him and Paige, she'd have to get it somewhere else. Whatever Emily had shared with her about his relationship was enough. He'd have to tell his mother to knock it off. He'd just as soon leave any conversation about his relationship off the table. Sadly, he thought it was off limits and hated the thought of rehashing the drama of it. It was long over, and he didn't want to revisit the memories anytime soon. Besides, there was a bus to drive.

Chapter Two

❧❦❧

The inkling that something was off didn't occur to Darcy until she was an hour into her Tuesday morning, sitting at the kitchen desk inside the Blueberry Point Lodge kitchen, ankles crossed, and staring at the schedule book. Beyond Friday, the calendar was blank.

Darcy leafed through the coming weeks, into October and November—not peak season, but still—and noticed the erasure marks. Save for two big Saturday events—a retirement party in two weeks and the wedding during the first weekend in October—everything else was wiped clean. All October weekends had been booked and at least five weekend events lined up for November, too, when she'd looked before Labor Day weekend. She pushed away from the desk and walked to the foyer, pausing at the bottom of the stairs.

"Ingrid?"

Ingrid Callahan had yet to make an appearance. It wasn't unusual that Darcy hadn't seen her employer yet this morning, but the lingering scent of Henry's cooking was noticeably absent too. She counted on Henry frying an omelet or homemade hash browns for their breakfast when she arrived each morning around seven thirty, something he still loved to do even after spending years as a cook at Del's in town. Stranger still was the missing to-do list. Ingrid left it on the desk for Darcy every morning.

No answer.

Darcy poked her head out the front door. The blue Explorer parked near the coach house's drive debunked the theory that Ingrid had run into town.

She shut the door, the click of the latch echoing in the airy space, and she immediately heard padded footsteps upstairs. Ingrid was here after all. Darcy swiped at a small web between the balusters as she waited for Ingrid to appear on the landing.

Instead, it was Henry. His thick, snowy hair spiked in every direction. Dark shadows underlined his eyes. She usually saw him dressed for the day at this hour, not wrapped in a flannel bathrobe.

"Good morning, Darcy. Ingrid's not feeling well today." He made no move to come all the way downstairs. Instead, he leaned against the wall as if standing took too much effort.

"Oh no. Is there anything I can do?" Darcy searched Henry's expression for a sign of how serious Ingrid's illness might be. He didn't look so well either. She paused. "I mean, aside from taking care of the cottages."

"We'll be okay." Then he snapped his fingers. "That reminds me. I forgot the list upstairs. I'll be right back."

Darcy noticed he moved slower than usual as he turned to go back upstairs, the soft hush of his loafers shuffling over the carpet. Though it was only September, the Callahans might have caught an early flu bug. She'd have to double up on the handwashing. She couldn't get sick, not with all that was on her agenda for the coming weeks. Her lists had begun sprouting sublists.

Five minutes later, as Darcy opened the door to head out to the first cottage, Henry's and Ingrid's voices again interrupted the silence. She strained to hear, but the sandstone brick house was well insulated with its foot-thick walls, and the labyrinthine hallways and two staircases leading up to the second floor muffled the noise. Again, she returned to the desk, waiting for one of them to appear and hopefully clear up the calendar conundrum.

A moment later Ingrid hustled down the stairs and into the kitchen as if she had escaped a crime scene. The woman was a hummingbird, constantly in motion. Yet Darcy still startled when Ingrid looped her arm with Darcy's and whisked them through the kitchen and into the front parlor with its lemon-hued walls.

"I don't want him to hear me," she whispered when she stopped near one of the huge windows, which lent an impressive view of the Big Lake. "He acts like I'm the sick one." Ingrid cast a glance through the kitchen toward the back staircase, the skin pinched between her eyebrows. Then with her lip trembling, Ingrid bowed her head. Her shoulders shook.

Darcy took both of her hands to calm her. "Ingrid? What's wrong?" She gave Ingrid the once-over as if it was that easy to determine. She certainly didn't look sick. On the contrary, Darcy hoped she looked as fit in thirty-five years as Ingrid did. What was Henry talking about? She led her boss over to the antique claw-footed couch. Ingrid sank onto the velvet cushions with a wavering breath.

"He doesn't want me to say anything, but I don't see how I can't." With a shaky hand, Ingrid brushed a stray gray curl off her forehead. She glanced at Darcy, her brown eyes lingering for a second on Darcy's, and in that moment Darcy knew this somehow affected her too.

"It's his heart again. I told you we had an appointment with the specialist on Friday afternoon." She gazed out the window to the lake and shook her head. "Well, he'll have surgery again next month. There will be months of rehab." She took one of Darcy's hands, patted it. "I can't do this alone. I'm too old for this."

"I'm here, Ingrid. I can help. You don't even have to pay me extra. I'm serious. Any hour that you need me, just call."

Ingrid's eyes grew sympathetic. "You've been great, honey. Really, I couldn't have hired a better person to oversee everything." She paused, carefully weighing her next words, and the spot of doubt, which had planted itself in Darcy's chest a minute ago blossomed into full-fledged trouble when Ingrid's steady gaze rested on Darcy. "I think we've decided to close Blueberry Point Lodge to guests. To sell."

Her new car. The apartment lease that she'd re-signed

last month. Her mom's constant innuendo that Darcy move back home and pursue her graduate degree in marine anthropology. These thoughts popped into her consciousness as soon as Ingrid said the word "close." Darcy hated herself for it because Ingrid and Henry were such sweethearts, the closest she had to family in Hendricks. They'd helped her adjust to the lakeside community when she'd been new to town last summer. Henry scouted garage sales to help furnish her place. Ingrid asked her to the monthly art co-op meeting of which Ingrid was president, and a gifted contemporary painter. They invited her to have dinner with them in Dentsen or Two Rivers a couple times a month. Now she only thought about how the Callahans' news would inconvenience her as the couple faced a medical crisis. *Get over yourself.*

But it was more than an inconvenience. Where would she find another job that paid so well? In season, Hendricks drew thousands. But November through March, Lake Superior's north shore was a frozen wonderland. An *empty* frozen wonderland. She dreaded the thought of leaving the place she'd grown to think of as home.

"Darcy?" Ingrid's concern creased her forehead.

Darcy tried to smile, but if felt lopsided, insincere.

Ingrid wilted against the back of the couch. "I'm sorry. I know this is a shock."

That snapped Darcy back. "No, don't apologize. Please." She rested her hand on top of Ingrid's. They were so cold, the skin so papery thin. "Henry needs major surgery. He's your priority. Not me, not this place. It's okay. I'll be fine."

The floor creaked upstairs and they looked at the ceiling. Ingrid shook her head. "He tried talking me out of it. He knows how much I love it here."

"You both worked hard to make it happen. I mean, aside from the community center, where else is there a place for a wedding reception if you don't want to go to Duluth or get eaten by bugs at the park pavilion?"

"True." Ingrid smiled then looked at her with earnest. "There are two events that I didn't have the heart to cancel —the retirement party for Henry's brother and the October wedding for the Osgoods, close friends of ours. I'm not sure how involved I can be. That being said, would you consider overseeing—"

"Of course."

Ingrid raised her hand. "Know that I'm planning to pay you through that wedding. Think of it as severance pay. That should give you time to find something else."

Darcy didn't know what she could possibly find here that would allow her to stay in Hendricks. Unless she worked three jobs, she didn't foresee even making half of what she needed each month. Putting applications in at the shipwreck museum and the lighthouse might be related to her history and anthropology majors, but she'd bet they were minimal-paying jobs, *if* they were hiring.

Ingrid laid her hand on top of Darcy's. "I do have a job lead for you."

Did she articulate her thoughts just then? It was no shock that Ingrid seemed to read her mind. She had a tendency to do that. Nevertheless, Darcy waited for Ingrid to continue.

"Now, don't dismiss this right away. I know it's not Blueberry Point Lodge, but it has the same opportunity to direct local events."

In her mind, Darcy was already shaking her head. She knew where Ingrid was going.

"I heard there's an opening for a tour host at...Sturgeon Widows Tours."

Darcy snorted unintentionally, a half-humor/half-derisive sound that she couldn't control. Her mother scolded her constantly for being too expressive about everything. She would admit it was a fault of sorts, but discretion wasn't part of her genetic makeup. Mom was clipped from the same fabric whether or not she'd admit it.

"I thought it was strictly a small family-run business?" Darcy got up from the couch to refill her coffee from the tea cart near the window. Her eyes bugged out when she turned her back to Ingrid. How was she going to get out of pursuing this lead? Ingrid was sweet to be concerned but—

"Emily Stetman runs everything. Trent, her husband, and younger son, Matt, are virtually hands off these days. I think Emily prefers it that way." She rolled her eyes. "Trent has been wanting to retire for the last five years, so he's essentially checked out. And Matt, well, he's always been a sweet kid. Funny too. But somewhat useless. At least that's what she tells me."

"She told you her own kid is useless?" If Emily Stetman talked about her own son so negatively, Darcy was sure she wouldn't want to work there. Who knew what kind of toxic atmosphere she'd be walking into?

Ingrid dismissed that with a small wave. "Emily and I

have known each other since the third grade. We used to be the best of friends." A sheepish grin brightened her face. "That is, until Henry moved to town in junior high."

Darcy laughed. "You and Henry were junior high sweethearts? I didn't know that."

"Never broke up. Not even for a day."

"I love that."

"It is pretty unusual, I'll admit." She leaned forward. "Anyway, back to your job prospects. Emily's other son, Sean, is...was...is the tour host. His schedule has been sporadic because of some personal issues. Emily says he needs a block of time off to recover fully, I guess."

"Personal issues?" Darcy asked hesitantly.

Ingrid's mouth dipped at the corners. "Relationship troubles."

"Wow. That must have been some breakup." Darcy crossed her arms. "I'm not sure I want to replace the owner's son. It sounds like a lot of drama." Here she was again, shutting the door as Ingrid handed her an opportunity. She mentally zipped her lips. *Just listen, Darcy.*

"I wouldn't look too far into it. It's a great opportunity. I don't know too many of the tour details, but I do know part of the tour involves the old shipwreck near the Clearwater Lighthouse."

Shipwrecks set her heart humming. Ingrid knew that too. Her former professor at the Southeast Michigan Maritime Institute had proposed a research project to her while she looked at graduate school last summer. The shipwrecks in Lake Superior were notorious, and they stirred an excitement that begged her to pursue her master's someday. So while leading tours wasn't exactly post-graduate studies, the chance to talk about shipwrecks and get paid for it might not be a bad gig after all. At least she'd be employed while she sorted out what she wanted to do next.

"Okay, Ingrid. You've talked me into it. How can I get in touch with Emily?"

Ingrid pulled a yellow slip of paper from the pocket of her cardigan. "Here's her number."

Darcy smiled at the wiliness of her boss. "Look at you. So ready to get rid of me," she teased, taking the note. She sat down again next to Ingrid.

"Darcy," Ingrid said in a chastising tone. "You know better than that. I would have kept you on forever if Henry's health didn't demand my full attention." As if on cue, they heard Henry opening a drawer in the kitchen, sifting through the silverware, and Ingrid put her finger to her lips. "He doesn't want to close the business, thinks he'll be back up for it after this next surgery."

Still fingering the paper in her hands, Darcy shook her head. "Even I know how impossible that would be. With all of the maintenance he did here all by himself? No way."

"Exactly. He doesn't know I'm talking to you about it. I told him we'd think it over and talk more later. It won't be easy, the letting go. So you understand?"

"Of course I do. I'll just miss this place. You guys too."

Ingrid rubbed Darcy's forearm. "We're not leaving Hendricks, just downsizing. We can still visit, right?"

"Yes, we can still visit." Darcy leaned toward Ingrid for a

reassuring hug, the scent of the older woman's lavender soap filling her nose.

Ingrid rose from the couch. "I think I'd better go see what all the silverware rattling means. It sounds like he's getting ready to cook something."

"It probably makes him feel useful." Darcy got up from the couch, too, intending to continue with her day as if this conversation hadn't taken place. Despite Ingrid's reassurance that she would be working for another month until the Osgood wedding, Darcy already felt disconnected. Her feelings must have registered on her face because Ingrid stopped on her way to the kitchen.

"I know it's not the best news, Darcy. But there's a bright side, honey. I know it. You just have to be on the lookout." Ingrid made her way to the kitchen to see what her restless, heart-weakened husband was up to.

Darcy smoothed the couch cushions and fluffed the two crimson tasseled pillows, tossing them back into each corner. What was the bright side in all of this?

She crossed the room again to gaze out at the lake. The water was angry today, the waves frothing as they hit the shore a short distance away from the rock-walled patio outside the window. On the warmest days in July, she loved to sit on the patio and feel the sun baking the stone, radiating that heat all around her while she sipped Ingrid's peach raspberry tea during her lunch break. She loved leading a group through the small patch of timber to the east of the property for blueberry picking. And she loved planning the events, especially weddings, attending to every detail for the people that entrusted Blueberry Point Lodge with their milestone parties. Now it was over. She was on her own.

As she stood before the window, Darcy searched for something positive in the situation. It certainly wasn't in the backyard of Blueberry Point Lodge or on the lake that churned like it felt her despair. Not anymore.

Chapter Three

✿❁✿

Two days later, Darcy grabbed the table in the large bay window area at Debi's Donuts. On Tuesdays and Thursdays before work, she'd get up a half hour earlier and skip breakfast so she could treat herself. She loved coming into Debi's with the sweet scent of baked goods and the rich aroma of coffee filling the small shop. She'd sit at the table alone with her cinnamon raisin Danish or an apple fritter, the special of the day, depending on the day of the week, and a coffee, to read a week's worth of Hendricks news from newspapers stuffed into the wall rack near her table.

She loved the lake in all of its serene, tempestuous, mysterious, unpredictable states. Growing up in the northern Chicago suburbs, her family had first visited the lake during the summer she was seven, renting a house with a small plot of beach access near Dentsen. They returned every summer after that until her father's death eight years later. Now living near it and seeing it daily was a different experience; it had grown familiar and a source of comfort for her, like an old friend.

The rush of air that swept the curls off her forehead when the front door opened interrupted her thoughts. It was Bethany, breezing into the shop like the wind that preceded her arrival through the door. Her willowy friend crossed the space with fluid grace gained from a longtime obsession with yoga and before that, childhood ballet lessons. She had recently opened her own yoga studio on Main Street.

Bethany pulled out the chair and collapsed in the seat, dumping her canvas bag onto the floor. "Hey there. Sorry I'm late." She tucked her shoulder-length bob behind both ears. "Silda darted out the door after a squirrel when I was leaving. Luckily, cats don't like to be wet. I didn't think it was going to rain today."

Darcy glanced at the sky outside the window. "It'll be done by noon." She pushed the vegan blueberry scone across the table toward her friend. "Debi is brewing more coffee. It should be ready by now."

As if on cue, Debi Thomas came from behind the counter with their mugs. "Hot and fresh."

Bethany's whirled around to look at the door. "Where is he?!"

"Just coffee," Debi said, chuckling. "The day I start stocking men in the pastry case is the day I'll have lines out the door and into the next county."

Darcy laughed and nudged her friend's hand. "There you go. New business venture." Bethany was always on the lookout for her next ex-boyfriend and joked about offering a men-only yoga class. Darcy quickly quashed that idea, reasoning that the type of men Bethany found attractive weren't the type who would take a yoga class in Hendricks.

Darcy waited until Debi was back behind the counter before she leaned across the table. "So I got some bummer news on Tuesday. Ingrid and Henry are closing Blueberry Point Lodge."

"No! Seriously?"

"I wish I weren't serious. Henry needs another operation. There will be a long recovery time again, and Ingrid isn't up for going it alone."

"Understandable. That's a big place, even for you two dynamos." She reached across the table to pat Darcy's hand. "I'm so sorry."

Darcy shrugged. "I can't dwell on it too long. I have to find something else and fast."

"Is it too soon to ask if you have any leads?"

"Well, Ingrid was a sweetheart to actually give me a lead after she broke the bad news." She thumped the file folder on the table beside her plate. "My resume. She said the tour company down the street is looking for a guide."

"Sturgeon Widows Tours?" Bethany asked with a half-amused expression.

Darcy could barely keep from smiling herself. "Hey, it's a job. And there's a lot of history behind the tour, I hear. I love that kind of stuff. It's just that...that thing on the top of the bus."

Some tourist towns had well-known landmarks or businesses with gimmicks. In Melton, an hour west, there was the abandoned mental hospital that was advertised as the most haunted place in the area. In Riverdale, just outside of Duluth, the Two Rivers Brewing Company bought goats to graze on top of their restaurant's grass roof. And then there were the two Sturgeon Widows Tour buses in Hendricks. Darcy would bet her brand-new Jeep that they could be spotted from outer space because of the hideous fiberglass sturgeons resting atop the gaudy vehicles. If Darcy wasn't desperate, there was no way she'd consider boarding one of those, let alone working on one.

Bethany nodded. "I get that. You wouldn't catch me driving around with a colossal plastic fish on my car roof."

Darcy sank against her seat back with exaggerated despair.

"There's a bright side in all of this, you know." Bethany lowered her voice in a conspiratorial tone.

"Please tell me," Darcy said, dabbing the crumbs from the corner of her mouth. "I've been wondering if any good can come from losing my job, but can't seem to find one."

Bethany's sat back in her chair and studied Darcy, a slow smile dawning on her face. "Well. There's Sean Stetman."

Darcy let out a breath. "Emily Stetman's son, right? The one with the issues? Never met him."

"Oh, you will. Believe me when I say he is perfection to the 'p.'"

"Haven't you tried setting us up before? I vaguely remember that you had."

Bethany looked at her underneath her lashes. "Yes, and you've not been taking me up on it," she purred. "You'd be perfect for each other."

Of course Bethany's bright side would involve a guy. To Darcy, that would be another negative. She didn't need any distractions as she struggled to stay afloat: starting a new job, paying bills, and proving to her mother that she didn't need to live at home to survive. Besides, most of the guys she dated found her too opinionated if they managed to stick around after the second date. It was usually at that point that she'd found fault with them first. Admittedly, Darcy was picky.

Darcy set her mug down. "Really, Bethany? You think I should get involved with the owner's son at my new job? A job that I haven't even accepted yet?"

Bethany looked at her with a blank expression. "I don't see the problem with that scenario."

Darcy could only chuckle. Of course she couldn't. Bethany was a serial dater, whereas Darcy had trouble connecting with guys. Aside from her discerning tastes in who she dated, she really dreaded the small talk as the precursor to developing a deeper relationship. She found it exhausting. For that reason, she avoided most of the guys who approached her. Bethany tried to set her up constantly, to no avail.

Despite her and Bethany's differences, Darcy counted Bethany as one of the most generous and positive people she knew. She was unselfish without fail, having given Darcy a complete bed set she bid on at an auction house in Dentsen, and a kitchen table and chairs she'd only bought a few months after Darcy moved to Hendricks. Bethany's parents, both attorneys in Minneapolis, still direct deposited a healthy monthly allowance into her checking account, even though their only daughter graduated college five years earlier. It was more than enough to supplement the small profit she made from her fledgling studio, and Bethany happily passed along the excess to whatever cause—or whoever—caught her attention.

But despite Bethany's general goodwill, Darcy had no intention of taking her up on relationship advice. In that area, Bethany lacked common sense and good judgment. Her past boyfriends had been too numerous to count in the eight years Darcy had known her. She was quick to commit and even quicker to get bored. Luckily, most had not been worth keeping, in Darcy's opinion. The common denominator of all her prospects was an art for flattery, Bethany's weakness.

"It's getting late. I'm supposed to be there at ten," Darcy said, checking her phone.

"So if you haven't formally accepted the job, what are you doing this morning?"

Darcy slipped the resume file back into her bag. "The phone interview was yesterday, but today I'm supposed to ride the route to get a sense of what it's all about."

"I bet Sean's driving you around," Bethany said, waggling her eyebrows.

"No interest."

"You wait and see."

They cleared their table of empty mugs and napkins then stopped outside on the sidewalk. Darcy gave her friend a hug.

"Thanks for being here."

Bethany shrugged. "What do you mean? We always do Thursday mornings."

"No, I mean thanks for being around for me to vent."

Bethany's eyes softened. "See, aren't you glad I talked you into moving to Hendricks? You may not have a job, but you have me."

IF HER NERVES RIPPLED DURING HER PHONE interview yesterday, Darcy's anxiety swelled like storm-churned waves after she parked her car at the curb. She lifted her bag onto her shoulder and climbed the short set of stone steps that led to the walled patio in front of Sturgeon Widows Tours. An identical yet much smaller version of the sturgeon replica atop the tour buses hung on the sign beside the front door. The air still had a bite to it despite the sun hanging in the midmorning sky, unhindered by clouds. She caught sight of her reflection in the glass door as she opened it and decided she looked composed enough, despite her nerves.

The lobby was empty except for two women studying a computer screen behind the counter. They both looked up with fleeting smiles, but their attention was clearly on the screen before them. One of them held up a finger, presumably meant for Darcy, but she didn't say anything for a full thirty seconds.

Finally, the older woman with a hairdo of spun sugar and a wide, red-lipped smile, came around the counter, holding out her hand. "Darcy Conti? I'm Emily Stetman. How do you do?"

Darcy received the woman's cool, firm handshake. "Fine, thanks. It's nice to meet you."

Emily swept her hand toward the other woman, who now Darcy could see was several years younger than herself. "Darcy, this is Melina Pereja, our business manager."

The younger woman's gaze bore into her when Darcy looked her way. Hers wasn't a friendly face. In fact, Melina Pereja looked downright unhappy Darcy was there.

"Nice to meet you," Melina said simply. To Emily, she said, "I'll try to work through this some more if you want to talk with her."

"Great. I'm no help with those computer issues anyway." She led Darcy to an office off the lobby and ushered her in. Closing the door, she offered Darcy a seat in a high-backed swivel chair. Emily sat opposite her in an upholstered wingback with threadbare arms. Darcy handed her the resume from her bag, and Emily took it, simultaneously studying it and nodding.

"I can see why Ingrid recommended you for this. Aside from overseeing Blueberry Point Lodge, you were a history and anthropology major. Oh, and at SEMMI too. My husband, Trent, went there." She glanced up at Darcy. "Tell me a little about your internship with the Great Lakes Naval Exploration Group. Sounds fascinating."

Darcy cleared her throat. "It was. I spent the summer cataloging artifacts from a shipwreck near Marquette. Tedious work, but I loved it."

"I can understand why," Emily said. "We have a shipwreck site on our tour. The *Lianthia* near Clearwater

Lighthouse. On calm days, you can see the hull near the surface."

"Yes, I've seen it."

Emily rummaged around on the desk beside her, grumbling under her breath about cleanliness. "Sorry, this is my son's desk. I have no idea how he can function with a work area like this."

While Emily hunted for whatever was hidden in the messy recesses of the desk, Darcy scanned the office. A collection of caps hung from a primitive rack on one wall. The September page of a calendar hanging on the wall displayed a watercolor painting done by a local artist Darcy recognized. Framed photos of people wearing fishing vests and waders holding huge fish decorated another wall. Darcy noticed a very good-looking guy appearing in most of the photos, his face shadowed by a hat. She could tell it was the same person by his stance—confident, broad-shouldered, long-legged. She bet that was Sean.

"Aha!" Emily pulled a folded map out from under a formidable pile of papers, maps, and tourist brochures. Several tumbled to the floor, but she ignored them. "You'll need this. It covers all of Broman County. We don't tour too far outside the county limits."

Darcy took the map. She wanted to ask if the guy in the photos was her son Sean, but Emily talked without pause.

"We have an eleven o'clock tour scheduled today. A lunch group. There will be an hour tour beforehand, starting west of Hendricks. Then a lunch stop at Red's Tavern and ending at the Harvest Garden pergola south of downtown near the pier. We're hosting a gardening club from Duluth. I thought you'd like to ride along to observe."

She could only nod before Emily continued with the day's itinerary.

"Now, understand that Melina will be leading the tour." Emily lowered her voice. "It's not her thing, to tell you the truth. It might get…awkward. That's why I need you to get up to speed very quickly." She snapped her fingers twice in quick succession to apparently emphasize how fast Darcy needed to comply.

"What happened to the previous tour guide?" Darcy thought she might get more information if she pretended she hadn't heard Ingrid's cryptic explanation about Emily's son needing time off. It was a legitimate question to ask, right? She didn't want to appear nosey.

Emily folded her hands in her lap. "Honestly, my son Sean was the tour guide. He's going through some personal issues and just doesn't have the energy for such a high-profile job." She looked down, twisting the ring on her finger. "He just needs a little break." Her voice dwindled during the last few words.

So this wouldn't be a permanent job. Would she be let go as soon as her son recovered?

The older woman looked up and seemed to sense Darcy's uncertainty. "We haven't run both buses simultaneously in a long time. At least two years. And lately, we really could use both with as busy as it's been. If…when Sean is ready to assume the guide role, I think it's entirely possible that we'll have room for two guides. We're even thinking of taking the business into new directions."

Emily stood up. "Since it's getting close to eleven, why don't you go mingle with some of the guests?" She peered through the office door. "Yes, I see that they're here already. Melina should be out there too."

"Sounds ideal. Thanks so much," Darcy said, shaking Emily's hand.

"If you have any questions while you're out, Melina will be able to answer them."

Darcy left the office and found her way outside again, tucking the map and tour itinerary into her bag. Melina leaned against the patio's stone wall, studying a green binder with the Sturgeon Widows Tour fish logo on the front. When she noticed Darcy approaching, Melina shut the book.

"All ready for the grand tour?" Melina asked.

"I think so."

"Did Emily tell you what a terrible guide I am?"

Darcy guessed her face registered the shock at such a direct question because Melina waved her off. "No worries. It's common knowledge around here. I'd so rather be back in the office it's not even funny."

"I'm sure you're a great tour guide."

Melina laughed. "Don't be ridiculous. I suck."

The conversation reminded Darcy again of how much she detested small talk, especially when Melina's gift for conversation seemed as nonexistent as her own. If Melina liked fishing for compliments, she wouldn't get them from Darcy.

Nearby, a car door closed. Darcy turned to see the guy who owned a black Silverado cross between the truck and her car. He made his way up the stone steps, taking them two at a time. He approached them unaware, head ducked and his face shadowed by a ball cap. It must have been Sean Stetman. There was no mistaking the man coming toward her compared to the figure she'd seen in the photos, but the ball cap was a dead giveaway.

"Hey, stranger," Melina called.

He startled and stopped, acknowledging Melina with an abrupt nod before his gaze settled on Darcy.

He opened his mouth, and an unintelligible word escaped him.

She stared at him for several awkward seconds, wondering what he'd said. Should she ask him to repeat himself? She stood there stupidly, wondering what to do as if she'd never met anyone before.

"Hello," he said. He touched the brim of his hat and then hurried past them into the lobby.

"Hi," Darcy said toward his retreating back, balling her fists at her side. *Stupid!*

Melina whispered, "That's Sean, Emily's son. He's been going through a tough time the last few months. Best to steer clear of him if you can."

Darcy watched him disappear inside. Yes, she had seen him around town. Bethany was right. His well-known personal problems notwithstanding, Sean Stetman was very easy to look at.

Melina glanced at the bus. "Listen, we'd better get everyone rounded up and on the bus. It's a pretty tight schedule, so we literally have to watch the minutes." She stopped to leaf through her binder, clearly flustered as she searched for something. "Would you mind steering folks onto the bus? I forgot something inside. Be back in a minute," she said.

Darcy watched Melina cross the patio, taking short, purposeful strides before she disappeared back inside the lobby too. She looked up at the bus and groaned inwardly at the sight of the monstrous fiberglass fish peering over the roofline at her. She couldn't really call it a bus—it didn't look like one with that—that *thing* on the top.

"Hideous," she mumbled under her breath. No amount of head-ducking or averted glances would hide the fact she was about to board that rolling fish wagon voluntarily and pretend she loved it.

"Wait for us!"

Four women hurried across the patio, Styrofoam cups of coffee in hand, sending steamy clouds trailing behind them.

One of the women huffed, out of breath. "Sorry. Last-minute bathroom stop," she said, holding up her drink. "Too much coffee already."

Darcy smiled. "Good thinking. Are we ready for the grand tour?"

"Are you the driver?" another woman asked. She wore a green sun visor and matching Keds.

"No, I'm the one with all the answers."

The four of them looked confused, and Darcy groaned inwardly. They never understood her sarcasm. She shrugged. "You definitely don't want me driving. I'm Darcy, your tour-guide-in-training."

While the visor lady's mouth shaped itself into an "O" in tentative understanding, the others at least smiled at her joke. Darcy mentally shook her head. Until she found her tour-giving groove, she'd keep her special brand of humor under wraps.

She boarded the bus behind the women to take a head count and match it to her copy of the tour manifest. There should have been twenty-four in all, maximum capacity for the custom-built bus. After confirming all guests were aboard, Darcy took a minute to study the bus interior. Despite the gaudy fish on the top, the inside was eclectic, a happy surprise. Maybe because green was her favorite color (the seats) or that she was drawn to mixed media art (the decoupage walls) justified why she liked it. If only they'd ditch the hideous fish.

She sat down next to a lady with a canvas floral bag on her lap.

"We should be on our way in a minute or so," Darcy said. "We're just waiting for the driver and, well, the tour host." She hesitated, not knowing if she should say anything more. She really didn't want to go looking for them, but it was past eleven o'clock. This wasn't good for business.

"Feel free to refill your coffee too." Darcy pointed to the red carafe at the built-in drink station behind the driver's seat. "Then we'll get started." She glanced toward the office, hoping the door would open and Melina and Sean would finally make their appearance.

When they had yet to appear five minutes later, Darcy reluctantly stood up. "It appears we're not quite as ready as I thought we were. My apologies. I'll be right back."

If she'd been employed for longer than an hour, she might lecture Melina on the importance of first impressions.

That Melina and the owner's son, personal drama aside, were late, even by a couple minutes, set a bad precedent. Darcy strode across the patio again, taking a deep breath before opening the door to the office.

Inside the lobby, the air crackled with tension. Melina stood in front of Sean with her arms crossed. She made eye contact with Darcy over his shoulder, gave her a shadow of a smile, but was clearly not about to interrupt the conversation to speak with her.

Darcy reasoned there was no time to be polite. Their guests waited on the bus. The tour should have begun ten minutes ago. If she learned one thing in the community college tourism class she took last winter, thanks to Henry and Ingrid paying for some "professional training," it was that clients come first. And leaving them waiting on the bus was just plain rude.

"Excuse me."

Melina's eyebrows arched at Darcy's intrusion.

"Everyone is waiting on the bus. Shouldn't we be on the road by now?"

Emily came out of the office, visibly upset. "He told me he'd be here, Sean. He didn't call you?"

The urgency Darcy felt vanished when the man before her—owner's son, heartbreak victim, tour driver oblivious to his paying guests—suddenly wheeled around and glared at her. His supposed fragile mental state was causing a not-so-small dilemma in the Sturgeon Widows Tours lobby, and he glowered at *her*?

Sean turned around again. "No, he didn't," he answered flatly.

"I'm so sorry," Emily said, pleading with her eyes. "I hate this, but...could you drive? I promise you can have an extra day off after this."

"I was supposed to have many days off. Melina can drive," he said, pronouncing every syllable with clear annoyance.

"She's giving the tour. Remember?"

"I can drive," offered Darcy. It didn't sound like anyone else was capable, so *why not?*

Emily opened her mouth to respond and froze. Melina, too, looked at Darcy in horror.

Sean slowly turned around again to study her with a silent, steady gaze. He took off his hat, which had shielded most of his face when she'd seen him on the patio, and his tawny hair fell askew across his forehead. To his credit, his eyes lost their sharp edge when he saw her, and his was such a sweeping glance over Darcy, head to toe, that an infusion of warmth made Darcy fan her face with the tour manifest. His heavy-lidded look, half indifference mixed with an intense curiosity caught her off guard, and any thought of insisting the Stetmans take her up on her offer to drive disappeared.

Melina broke the spell. "Let's get back to the guests," she said, hooking her arm through Darcy's. The young woman swept Darcy out the door without waiting for an answer.

"I don't think we need to witness that," Melina said when they were outside again, crossing the patio. "Sean and Emily haven't been very happy with each other lately."

"No kidding."

Melina stopped in front of the bus. "I know this isn't the best first impression of us. Really, it's a fun place to work. I think you'll like it." Then she looked back at the front door. "I'd just steer clear of Sean."

Darcy wondered if working at Sturgeon Widows was a good idea after all. Alarm bells told her there were some pretty major issues to sort out between Emily and her son. Whatever it was, Darcy hoped their drama wouldn't affect her.

Chapter Four

❧❦❧

Sean knew this would happen. He'd specifically asked his mother for a little time off, a break for him to get away and clear his head. Matt covered for him last week while Sean escaped to the cabin, and was supposed to drive this tour, too, since Sean had gotten back late last night. Of course Matt blew it off and decided to take another job without telling him. It was so typical of his younger brother that Sean questioned how Matt could function as an adult living on his own.

Emily pinched the skin between her eyebrows, a sign that one of her migraines wasn't far off.

"I know this is hard for you," she said. "You and Paige were so close."

Sean stuffed his hands in his front pockets and glowered at her. "I don't want to talk about that. That was months ago."

"Yes, but it's still affecting you."

"Please stop."

She sighed. "Fine. But what's the solution now? There is a bus full of people out there."

"I'm aware of that. One of them just came in here and offered to drive."

"What...drive? No, Sean, I—"

He held up his index finger. "I'll do it. But it doesn't make me happy. In fact, every time I have to cover for him, the resentment grows a little more." He smoothed his hair back before he slapped his cap back on and hurried out of the office. If he stayed in there one minute longer he'd suffocate.

Melina and that curly-haired guest who'd offered to drive stood outside of the bus talking. When they saw him coming, Melina climbed the steps into the bus, and it looked like the other woman would follow, but as he neared, she stopped and faced him. She stuck out her hand.

"I'm Darcy Conti," she said. Her voice was husky, which he hadn't expected. He also didn't expect to be enchanted by the almond-shaped eyes, dark-lashed and fierce at the moment. He'd only ever seen chestnut-colored eyes once, and they reminded him of his high school science teacher, Mrs. Dierk. He remembered being fascinated by their iridescence and their copper hue. When he finally returned Darcy's handshake, hers was a cool, firm grip.

"Sean Stetman." He glanced at the bus, and then back to her. "I think we're ready to go." He paused before adding, "And thanks, but I'll be doing the driving."

She looked at him blankly for a moment, then her brows drew together. If her eyes had been capable of firing ammunition, he'd be dead. He'd meant it as a joke, but it sounded awkward instead. She boarded the bus without another word, and he mentally kicked himself for being a jerk yet again. If he got through this day without drawing a bad review for the company, he'd count himself lucky.

Sean settled into the driver's seat, silently cursing the situation he now found himself in. His thoughts returned to the cabin as an escape; he needed a mental break. He'd made a point of telling his mother so. But with his father retired and his brother unreliable, there was no one to take over the workload. He turned the key into the ignition and Clem rumbled to life. In the overhead mirror, the faces of the guests bobbed above the high-backed seats, all of them focused on Melina as she gave the company safety spiel (no standing while the bus is in motion, no wading in water above your knees, blah blah blah). The mundane details of giving a tour had numbed his senses. He willed the time to fast-forward three hours.

That woman with the chestnut eyes sat two seats behind him. He caught her glaring at him twice in the short time they'd been on board. She held his gaze without the slightest ounce of self-consciousness, almost like a dare to be the one to look away first. Despite the black look she directed at him, she was pretty. Gorgeous, actually, in the fresh, outdoorsy way that always turned Sean's head. It had been a while since he'd looked at anyone with even the slightest interest, much to Melina's dismay.

Sean shook his head, clearing the crazy thought. *I'm not even going there.*

DARCY SHARED THE PLUSH GREEN SEAT WITH A middle-aged woman named Claire. They introduced themselves and segued into a conversation about the folk arts school near Dentsen. Sean kept catching her eye in his rearview mirror. If he was trying to intimidate her, it wouldn't work. She listened to Claire going on about the rug-hooking class she'd taken at Handmakery Folk School and Melina droning on about the history of their first stop at Red's Tavern. Emily was right; Melina was not cut out for giving tours. She'd put the entire bus to sleep if she didn't insert a little inflection into her presentation. Darcy put a hand to her mouth, feeling a yawn coming on.

If she weren't so desperate, she'd seriously consider not taking the job. Already the tense environment twisted her stomach into a knot, listening to the argument between Sean and his mother in the lobby. And Darcy never could compartmentalize her life like some people; she wished she could flip a switch once she left work, shutting off her professional life so she could relax. Whatever turmoil she faced at work tended to seep into her downtime as well. Melina's advice to avoid this Sean character was spot on. Talk about a miserable person.

On the bright side, the lake was breathtaking. A slight breeze caressed the lake, causing ripples to skitter across the surface closest to shore, cutting through the water like silver ribbons. Darcy stared out the window in between taking notes and looked forward to Saturday when she could take a book down to her favorite spot near the lake at Blueberry Point Lodge. An old red oak sat at the back of Ingrid and Henry's property with such an impossibly long reach that it stretched partly onto the beach. Darcy liked to plant a short folding chaise under it and read whenever she got the chance.

"Red's Tavern is basically a historic bar, er—" Melina glanced down at her notebook, clearly flustered. A few seconds later, she found her place again, reading it word for word, "—a historic watering hole for the men who worked the fishing industry in the late 1800s. By the way, what do you call a dangerous fish who drinks too much?"

The bus was silent with anticipation. Darcy cringed at Melina's awkward delivery.

Melina gave a short, barking laugh. "A beer-a-cuda!"

More groans than snickers from the crowd made Melina's smile falter when she didn't get the reaction she'd probably hoped for. If Melina wouldn't take herself so seriously and relax a little, she might have won over this bunch. Instead, Darcy hoped Melina would make it through the tour without bursting into tears.

Claire leaned over into Darcy's shoulder and whispered, "The poor dear should probably spend less time making jokes and more time practicing her lines."

Darcy smiled and turned to stare out the window again but felt a real urgency to learn the tour stops so she could spare Melina and Sturgeon Widows Tours any more embarrassment.

As Sean pulled the bus into the parking lot near the rustic clapboard building, Darcy ducked her head so she could see the new sign for Red's Tavern on top of the porch roof. The restaurant's owners had been making improvements during the last few months, and the gray-

and-black sign with red lettering was their newest addition. As many times as Darcy had eaten there with Ingrid and Henry, or Bethany, she'd never noticed just how charming it was, and she felt compelled to try seeing these tour stops as a guest for the first time.

Red's Tavern was renowned for its painted mural of a lake scene with white-sailed schooners. It covered the entire west wall of the building. White-and-green-striped umbrellas shaded four tables on the second-story balcony, which butted up against a basalt cliff at the rear of the tavern.

Darcy exited the bus with the rest of the guests and took a spot behind the others so she could watch Melina. She felt sorry for her. Though Melina gathered the group around her to give directions, the woman's forced smile was an easy read. She was totally out of her element.

"We'll be hearing from—" Melina started, flipping through her binder. "Shoot," she whispered, glancing at Darcy with panic in her eyes. "I've forgotten the name of who's talking with us today over lunch."

Darcy wanted to step in to, well, she didn't know what since she didn't have a copy of the script. If Melina kept screwing up, they'd get slammed with negative reviews for sure. But it was Sean, the last to leave the bus, who came up behind the group and eased his way into the situation.

"Red's Tavern is actually the oldest building in the county, built in 1887," he said, his voice taking on a clear, authoritative tone. "Part of the original building extends into the basalt rock of the cliff you see here. I think it's used as a storage area now. The rest of the building was constructed around it and rebuilt many different times due to fires, floods, and for some time, neglect, when it wasn't in operation for twenty years in the '60s and '70s."

"Was it always a tavern?" someone asked.

Sean shook his head. "It started as a watering hole for fishermen until the early 1900s, when the worst storm in the history of the Great Lakes flooded the area. Totally wiped it out. Then it was rebuilt as a supper club, then turned back to a tavern, then a little grocery store. It was even a laundromat until it partially burned in the early '60s."

He was clearly in HIS element. Darcy studied him while he engaged the group, and noted how his speech rang clear. He was nothing like the sullen person she'd seen inside the tour lobby. Something about his voice intrigued her, calmed her, stirred something in her. Sean's voice resonated in his chest, at once comforting, in control, deeply sensual.

Sean continued on. "And then Marvin and his wife Tonti Hill moved to Hendricks in the early '80s from Chicago after retiring from the restaurant business. But retirement didn't necessarily agree with them, especially when they saw the sorry shape this place was in."

A man standing near Sean nodded knowingly. "We're struggling with that same issue now," he said, and his wife smiled.

Sean clapped him on the shoulder. "Lots of former retirees on the North Shore. The small business opportunities up here are excellent."

The group laughed. Darcy checked on Melina and noticed she looked perfectly content hanging in the background, probably relieved she wasn't the center of attention any longer.

"Hey, Red!"

Sean waved to the big man who lumbered down the front steps of the tavern with two plastic bags for someone who'd just pulled up in a pickup truck. The man lifted his chin toward Sean in acknowledgement. He had a full head of flaming red hair.

"As you all can probably see, the name 'Red's Tavern' was not a coincidence," Sean joked, drawing laughs yet again. "Red's real name is Robert, and he is Marvin and Tonti's son. They named the place after their newborn son when they bought it. Let's head inside. They've set up lunch for us on the balcony."

Darcy quickened her steps to pass the group and get to Sean. His long, easy stride made her have to work twice as hard.

"You have a really engaging style."

Sean turned his head to look at her, like he was waiting for the punch line.

"I mean, they really respond to you. How long have you been giving tours?" Darcy saw her reflection in his aviator glasses and brushed the hair out of her face.

He stopped and pushed his glasses to the top of his head. "Since I graduated college. No, that's not right," he said, closing one eye to think. "Actually, I think I was a sophomore in high school when I did my first one."

"How long did it take you to develop your schtick?"

"My what?" he asked, the corners of his mouth lifting.

"Your schtick. You know, your routine."

"You're awfully interested in how the tour business runs. First you offer to drive the bus, now you want to know all of my secrets." He crossed his arms and leaned against the doorframe. The last person in the group moved past them and into Red's. "Are you looking to set up shop?"

"Absolutely not." Darcy felt her face flush. Then it dawned on her. Emily hadn't told Sean that Darcy was interested in covering for his leave. To Sean, Darcy was just a very curious tourist. Of course he would wonder about her intrusiveness. She needed to set the record straight.

"Maybe we should start over. I'm Darcy Conti."

"Yes, I remember. You introduced yourself an hour ago."

"I'm not on the tour as a guest. Your mother offered me the job to cover for you while you...while you're away."

He stared at her for an uncomfortably long time.

"Hello?" she finally said, waving her hand in his face.

He blinked. "You're going to take over the tours? Here?"

"Is that a problem?"

"No...no, not at all. That's great. I'm just surprised. I wasn't expecting...you."

Darcy felt like saying that he only had to come out of his cave long enough to listen to his mother. Melina mentioned he'd been absent lately, so it was understandable he didn't notice what was happening at Sturgeon Widows Tours. If he wasn't so busy wallowing in his funk, he might pick up on how much his mother had to take control of during his respite.

"Let me warn you: my brother will be a treat to work with."

"The one who didn't show up today? How so?"

His amusement brightened his eyes. "He'll try to take over. He won't be happy with just driving. My brother is every bit the life of the party."

"Why doesn't he lead the tours then?"

Sean scratched his neck. "He tried for a while but didn't really stay on topic. Then he started preferring construction jobs to leading tours."

Darcy laughed. "That's definitely a problem for a small company like this."

"Definitely," he said, a one-sided smile on his lips. "Listen, I'd better get back to the group. Sorry I didn't catch on earlier," he said, rubbing his hands together, looking like he'd rather be anywhere but talking to her.

Darcy shrugged. "Not a problem. Now that you know the truth, don't think I'm checking you out when you catch me hanging on your every word," she teased. "I'm just studying."

The hint of a smile disappeared. "I won't."

With that, he pulled open the screen door and walked into the tavern. Darcy watched him go, hanging back for a minute and wondering why she constantly sabotaged conversations. What she wouldn't give for an ounce of finesse sometimes. She'd just insulted the owner's son, who happened to need a mental health break. If she could keep her mouth shut for the rest of the tour, without stirring up one more awkward moment, maybe she'd have this job for longer than a day.

She had to make it work. And if Sean Stetman was going to be out of the office for the foreseeable future, that was fine with her. Maybe their personalities didn't quite mesh, but what did it matter? They wouldn't be working together. It sounded like his brother regularly drove the bus anyway. Well, when he showed up. Hopefully he'd show up.

The lunch, well suited to a group of gardeners, was locally sourced—salmon, herbed red potatoes, fruit compote, and glazed lavender spritzes. While the breakfasts that Henry whipped up for the cabin guests at Blueberry Point Lodge were fantastic, this lunch was definitely one that people would drive from Duluth to try. Maybe even the Twin Cities. *Mom would love this place*, Darcy thought, making a mental note to call her later. She was due for a visit soon anyway.

Nibbling on one of the lavender cookies, Darcy found a spot on one of the benches against the balcony railing and began making notes for herself about the morning stops. A short time later, Melina moved in next to her, sighing dramatically.

"I didn't make too big a fool out of myself, did I?" She put her hand up. "Wait. Don't answer that."

Darcy purposefully paused before she opened her mouth this time. "You weren't that bad," she said.

"Compared to him, though," Melina said, staring pointedly at Sean, who talked to a rapt audience across the way. The three women, at least twice Sean's age, hung on his every word. He was entertaining, but honestly, Darcy knew they weren't giddy only because of his outgoing personality. The simple gold henley shirt he wore stretched across his broad shoulders in a very enticing way. He looked like he worked out, and that reminded Darcy that she had NOT exercised in weeks. Maybe some time in Bethany's yoga studio wouldn't hurt. And speaking of Bethany, unfortunately she was right: Sean Stetman was quite easy to look at.

"Well, it sounds like he was giving tours while still in the womb. I wouldn't compare myself to him if I were you."

Melina huffed. "Oh, I'm not." She paused, still watching the group. She leaned in closer and whispered, "He's not interested now, but I think Sean and I would be a good match."

Darcy put her notes aside. "Oh?"

"I've hinted that I'd be interested when he starts dating again."

"His girlfriend must have really done a number on him."

Melina pressed her lips together. "I met her a few times. She wasn't very nice to him. Then the accident…"

"So…what happened to her?"

"I'm not sure exactly, car accident or something. She was in a coma for almost a month. Then stayed in the hospital quite awhile after that, followed by months of physical therapy. Sean helped her through most of it. Then she told him to get lost. Broke his heart—" Melina's voice trailed off. She hitched her shoulders. "It was rough for him."

Darcy's attention turned back to Sean. "Sometimes those traumatic losses never heal."

"He spends too much time alone, I think. If I could get him to open up a little more, I know he'd come around," Melina said. "No one is worth a lifetime of solitude."

Darcy thought of her own mother who had lost her husband when Darcy was fifteen. She remembered with painful clarity the morning her father had quizzed her for that day's biology exam at the breakfast table. That afternoon, in the midst of the exam, Mrs. Bartlett, the principal, had come into class. She'd spoken in a whisper to Darcy's biology teacher behind her hand. Darcy would never forget how their fleeting looks had settled on her at the same time, their eyes reflecting the life-altering news she had yet to learn. Darcy could still imagine the swish of Mrs. Bartlett's skirt, the clip of her heels echoing in the classroom, as if the sound had sucked the life from everyone else in the space, leaving her and Mrs. Bartlett alone. Her principal had put a hand on her shoulder.

"Follow me, dear," she had said, and when Darcy walked into the office moments later and saw her uncle Jason, his eyes ringed red, she'd known something horrible had happened. Carl Conti—a robust, former Navy colonel who competed in Iron Man competitions—collapsed during a meeting from a brain aneurysm. In the weeks after the funeral, Fran Conti, once an independent, gregarious business owner, had suddenly turned into a clingy, fearful woman. To Darcy's knowledge, her mother had yet to show any interest in dating.

She shook her head. "I wouldn't hold my breath. From what I saw in the lobby this morning, he's not ready."

Melina smiled with easy confidence. She apparently thought she was better at attracting guys than giving tours. "Don't worry. I'm pretty good at reading signals."

Darcy studied him again while she finished her cookie. "You'll know when he's ready, I guess. If you're bent on dating him."

Melina's brow dipped when she glanced at Darcy. "You don't think I should?"

"It's really none of my business, though I wouldn't date someone I work with. It hardly ever ends well."

As Darcy looked over her notes, her thoughts whirled around Sean and his apparent heartache. That would partly explain his behavior. Why she was giving so much thought to someone she'd met only two hours ago confounded her. Whatever issues Sean Stetman struggled with were none of her business. As only the company driver and one looking to take a leave of absence, he wouldn't interact with her much anyway, right?

Chapter Five

❧❀❧

The bus pulled up to Sturgeon Widows Tours promptly at three o'clock. Sean was exhausted. Having not planned to lead the tour, he wasn't mentally prepared. That cost him. For as good as he was at narrating, it always drained him. To recharge, he needed time to himself: a quiet meal, a little bit of television, a walk up the Sage River trail with Brandy, his golden retriever.

He followed the last person off the bus but was stopped by two women who gushed about the tour and the North Shore. He smiled politely, thanked them for taking the tour, then excused himself. He headed toward the building, keeping his head down to avoid eye contact so he could get to his office uninterrupted.

Emily poked her head out of the lobby door as he neared the building. He hoped his mother wouldn't read his takeover of the tour as a sign he wanted to come back to work. He'd clear that up as soon as possible but not in front of Melina and Darcy, who stopped ahead of him to talk with Emily. He squeezed in between the three women and walked briskly through the lobby, only pausing to check the message board behind the counter.

"How did the tour go?"

Sean turned to look at Emily, but the question was directed to the other two women. He caught Emily's eye over Darcy's shoulder and saw the slight frown creasing his mother's forehead.

"Sean was brilliant," Melina said. "I drove and he did the tour," she said, holding up her hand to stop Emily's questions. "I know. I tried, but I was seriously worried those ladies were going to stand up on the bus and demand their money back after the first stop."

Emily looked to Darcy. "That bad?"

He couldn't hear what Darcy said but she nodded slightly.

Emily's shoulders dropped. "I'm happy to hear it worked out."

He intended to grab his truck keys and go home, but Emily's words stopped him. Now was the time to reiterate his terms. He needed time off, a good chunk of time. Suddenly, a public confrontation with his mother was the least of his worries.

"I talked to Matt," she said, jumping in before he could speak.

He shook his head. The name "Matt" made his blood pressure skyrocket at the moment. He couldn't stand to hear another word.

Emily pressed her hands together apologetically. "He

said he couldn't turn the job down. I'm sorry, Sean." She winced. "He said driving is out of the question."

Sean couldn't speak. If he did, he doubted he could check his self-control. Instead, he stormed past them to get to his office. His desk was a mess and his keys weren't where he thought he'd put them. Patience gone, Sean picked up two handfuls of papers, brochures, maps, and who knew what else, and tossed them into a corner. The keys rattled somewhere, so he swept another pile into the opposite corner. There they were.

Leaving the paper-strewn office, he slammed the door closed. Darcy and his mother still stood together in the lobby, watching him with widened eyes. He breezed past them, but then stopped. He took two steps back until he was face to face with Darcy. Unblinking, she stared at him with a mixture of contempt and surprise. One eyebrow arced, seemingly to mock him.

"Looks like we'll be working together after all," he said flatly. She didn't say anything but continued to watch him, and really, what could she say when his anger was on full display? As he walked toward the door, he reasoned he'd misdirected his resentment toward Darcy, that it was his mother, and most definitely Matt, who deserved it instead. They should have had more options for tour hosts and drivers than just two people. But he wasn't thinking about defusing the situation at the moment. He'd apologize some other time.

Sean gave his mother one last withering look before he left through the lobby door.

LATER THAT NIGHT, SEAN SAT IN FRONT OF THE wood stove, drumming his fingers on the armchair and petting Brandy with his other hand. His mood still hovered around annoyed after hitting full-tilt furious at work, but the wood stove and his dog were his go-to stress relievers. Regret had begun to creep into his conscious too. His behavior at the office was unacceptable and irrational, so he stewed in his guilt. He knew if he wasn't Sean Stetman, part owner of Sturgeon Widows Tours, he would have been fired on the spot.

It was a little early in the season to fire up the stove, but the warmth on his face and the gold flames licking at the window was meditative. Brandy stretched her neck and leaned into the side of the chair to position herself to where his fingers would deliver the most satisfying scratch. He smiled at her skill of knowing exactly what she wanted and getting it. If only it were that simple for him.

Of course this all came back to Paige. He needed to get his head on straight so he could get back to living: giving the tours, helping grow the business, seeing friends. Admittedly, he'd turned into a recluse. Pathetic. He rubbed the sides of his face with his hands, feeling the gritty stubble on his skin.

Paige.

That name still made the anxiety pool in his chest. During the year they were together, Sean bet he was more familiar with Paige's retreating back than he was with her face. Had he known her passion for traveling from the start, he most likely wouldn't have been interested. It just wasn't something he was interested in at this point in his life. The business didn't allow it.

He and Paige had met through his best friend, Ryan, who had been trying to set up Sean and Paige for months. She was outdoorsy like Sean, Ryan said. They had hit it off immediately once they met, trading stories about fishing (the Sage River was their favorite) and arguing about where the sunsets were better: Clear Lake Point or on top of the watchtower in Tettegouche State Park.

They had a good six months together before he started to realize Paige was a very restless person. She wasn't good at sitting still. She was constantly on the go, though much of it was her freelance work as a photographer. With the traveling she did through her job, Sean was surprised she didn't want to take it easy on her off days.

Then her trip to India with her sister last year had lit a fire in her, and the inheritance left by her father helped fuel it. When she begged him to go with her, first to Belize, then Alaska, and finally Peru in late January, all over the course of several months, his resentment grew. How could she maintain that lifestyle? What plans did she have to pay for those trips when her money ran out? Granted, her photography skills were top rate. She'd been published in *Travel* and *National Geographic* and other big-name publications. He tried explaining the practicality of saving some, but she wouldn't hear it. The more Sean tried reasoning, the more she refused to listen.

You're selfish, she'd said. *You only think of your business. Everyone needs time off.*

It was an endless, circular argument that filled their

moments together until she left for the next trip. Finally what feelings he felt for her vanished too. It wasn't that she didn't love him. She did, and she told him often. Paige's need for space was greater, though. And eventually, Sean had enough.

The trouble with that realization though, especially for a quiet guy like himself, was that he let it simmer inside too long. It was never the right time or he just didn't want to bother—he valued the peace and quiet after hours of leading lovesick honeymooners or midlife married couples around, extolling the merits of Hendricks. The last thing he wanted to do after work was create tension. She accused him of picking fights, when in fact, she was the one who constantly asked him to leave his responsibilities behind. So he kept quiet. For months.

Then in the spring after she'd come back from backpacking the Colca Valley in the Andes, they'd had their biggest fight yet. Couldn't he take a week off at the end of May for a long weekend to Puget Sound? She had enough airline reward points to cover the cost of two tickets. They could stay at a bed-and-breakfast on one of the islands, hike, and fish. When he mentioned that Memorial Day weekend was the start of the busiest time of year for the tour company, Paige said he should leave her and date his job instead. He called her bluff, breaking up with her on the spot. The full Nalgene water bottle that she threw at his head, narrowly missing him, but shattering the antique mirror above his couch, was her answer. Before storming out, she grabbed one thing: her copy of *If You Could Travel the World,* heavily bookmarked with neon Post-its.

She said she'd come by in the next two weeks while he was at work to pack some of the things she'd kept at his cabin. Then a few days later, he took a call at work from her sister, Paula. It took a full minute before he could make out her words as she sobbed uncontrollably. Paige had been in a pedestrian accident in downtown Minneapolis. She was in a hospital there. It wasn't good. Wasn't good at all.

Paige lingered in a medically induced coma for nineteen days before she regained consciousness. He'd visited her bedside and consoled Paula and her mother while he camped out in the orange vinyl armchair in the corner of the room. Sean couldn't muster any concern when Paula and her mother fretted if Paige could continue her globetrotting lifestyle. What he felt was anger and resentment instead, and it shamed him. Why couldn't he empathize with them? Had she wrecked him enough that the anger smothered his once-loving feelings for her? He hated himself for it. So he withdrew.

The trouble with retreating, though, was that again he didn't talk to anyone about the whole ordeal—the breakup and his subsequent guilt. He confided in no one. For all his friends and family knew, she had broken up with him. He missed her, they thought. They had spent close to a year together. Of course he needed time. It wasn't healthy, letting these feelings simmer unchecked. But who would understand what he really felt was guilt, not grief. Guilt because he'd wanted their relationship to end so he could have peace again. Guilt because he couldn't tolerate being around her anymore, yet he didn't have the mindset to tell her. For that, their relationship ended horribly. He felt like a coward for avoiding the conversation they should have had. That they were too different, that maybe they should break it off. Amicably, and not with a plastic missile being hurled at his head. The relationship had left such a bad taste in his mouth that he couldn't think of starting another.

Brandy nudged his hand as if to tell him to get over himself, that he'd better get back to more important things, like scratching her. He chuckled at her single-mindedness and renewed his efforts.

"What do you think I should do? How do I get back on track?"

She tilted her head at the sound of his voice so she could look at him while still be in range of his fingers. She opened her mouth in a wide, doggy smile. If Brandy could speak his language, Sean knew her advice would be spot on. She seemed to sense he was thinking of her and circled her body around so she faced him, and her expression took on that earnest focus dogs excelled at. She let out a short woof, pawing at his chair.

"Believe it or not, life is a little more complicated than just figuring out how to get your neck scratched." He stopped his fingers, teasing her, and she nudged him. Relentless.

Until he straightened his head, he couldn't begin to think about another relationship. Then again, maybe he was better off alone. He had never been good at talking—well, aside from being "on" during the tours—and he knew he needed to work on that instead of shutting down when conflict came his way.

Thinking about conflict brought back the events at the

end of the day—the way he'd barked at their new employee, that Darcy woman. He'd start by apologizing. Yes, it would be the beginning of communicating in a more mature way and not like a petulant five-year-old. If it wasn't too late, maybe she'd forget his attitude from earlier and give him a chance to prove he wasn't a first-class jerk.

Chapter Six

✣

After witnessing the dynamics of the Stetman family last Thursday, Darcy doubted she could work in such a tense environment. She lay in bed Sunday morning fretting about it, wondering if she had made the mistake of accepting this job so hastily. After studying the tour guide all day yesterday, she knew she could handle the itinerary. In fact, she loved the idea of sharing the area's history with the guests. But that family! They needed to fix some serious issues before it affected their business. She had been spoiled at Blueberry Point Lodge, working by herself so much during her days there, and Ingrid and Henry were such sweethearts. Their interactions seemed based more upon a long-lasting friendship than a work relationship. She'd miss them terribly.

Rollie seemed to sense her unease. He crawled toward her from the foot of the bed, licking her chin when he was snuggled into the crook of her arm.

"What should I do, buddy? Should I stop worrying and work with that rotten Sean Stetman?"

Her dog looked up, cocked his head, and whined.

"I know. I don't want to either." She scratched the area between his two pointed ears, his favorite spot. His head followed her hand when she slowed down. "But someone needs to keep you in kibbles and rawhides."

Maybe she should keep looking. When she found something else, she'd put her notice in. If only she hadn't re-signed the lease on the loft. Rentals didn't move fast in Hendricks, so subletting was out of the question. In the meantime, she'd make the best of working with Sean Stetman. There was no denying he was extremely good-looking, an irrefutable positive in spite of his belligerence.

She was determined to have a slow, luxurious day after she went to give the two cabins a quick cleaning at Blueberry Point Lodge. Ingrid gave in to the family that had reserved the cabins months ago for a reunion. They'd offered to pay double the amount if Ingrid would let them keep their reservation. "How could I say no?" reasoned Ingrid. She had trouble saying no to anyone and anything. It was the last time Darcy would have to service the cabins, Ingrid promised.

An hour later Darcy pulled in front of the house and shut off the engine. Ingrid, an avid gardener, sat on her aluminum folding stool in the east garden, deadheading her Champlain roses. She heard Darcy close her car door and waved over her shoulder without turning, still focused on her flowers.

Ingrid bent at her waist, reaching for the darkened

blossoms, their petals curling inward. She snipped with a hushed precision—*snip, drop, snip, drop, snip, drop.*

"Are you ready for tomorrow?"

Darcy eased herself to the ground, and sat cross-legged by Ingrid's side. "I suppose."

"I don't hear the customary first-day-on-the-job excitement in your voice," Ingrid chided. She stopped clipping and faced Darcy. "Are you having second thoughts or something?"

Darcy smiled. "Or something."

"You must have met Sean. I hear he has that effect on people now."

"He's different, all right. I'm not even sure he's capable of driving, let alone narrating a tour."

Ingrid smiled. "He can be a piece of work. You should have seen him as a toddler. Oh my goodness, what a pill. In all fairness, he lost that girlfriend of his. That took a lot out of him from what Emily said."

"Yes, I've heard." Darcy took Ingrid's clippers and snipped some of the wilting blossoms nearest her.

"I'm glad I got to see you today. I wanted to tell you this in person." Ingrid looked sheepish. "And ask another favor."

"More bad news, Ingrid?"

"Well, not exactly. It's really nothing yet, but someone approached us about buying Blueberry Point Lodge."

"So soon? I'm not ready for you to leave here." After she said it, Darcy realized how selfish she sounded. "I don't mean that. I'll just miss you."

Ingrid gave her hand a reassuring pat. "I know you don't,

dear." She shrugged. "Henry and I really didn't think about it at all, but then we heard that someone we know is looking for a turnkey operation on the North Shore. I guess word got out that we're not booking anything anymore."

Darcy stopped deadheading. She scooped up some of the fallen heads and sifted them through her fingers, letting the petals fall to the grass. Another handful she brought to her nose, breathing in their sweet, pungent earthiness. It was all happening so quickly. She looked toward the lake, trying to imagine not having this place as a respite.

"Darcy?

"Sorry," Darcy said, handing her back the clippers. "My mind is other places today. What's the favor?"

"That's understandable, dear," Ingrid said, patting Darcy's hand. "This person is coming by in a bit for a little look-see. I'd really appreciate it if you stuck around and showed him the place. I'll be here of course, but you're so much better at that kind of stuff than I am."

"Of course I can help, Ingrid."

Suddenly her lazy Sunday afternoon was history, like those wilting Champlain blooms.

AFTER STRIPPING THE BEDSHEETS FROM THE BED and stuffing them into the canvas laundry bag on the small porch, Darcy locked the door on Cabin Two. Good timing. Behind her, the crunch of gravel signaled the arrival of Ingrid's potential buyer. She sighed. She wasn't ready to leave this place, let alone show it off to someone else.

The low, sleek car slunk up the drive and stopped in front of the expansive porte-cochere, which Ingrid always said was her most favorite part of the house. Only the grandest old homes had them, she said. Its sky-high roof and stone pillars made her feel like royalty. This stranger's car looked perfectly at home next to Blueberry Point Lodge. Even from a distance Darcy smelled money.

She ditched the canvas tote in the backseat of her car and went to meet the man as he stepped out of his ostentatious ride. Darcy didn't need to see its price tag to know it cost much more than what she made in a year. She could tell by the car's profile. Ingrid came down the steps off the back patio at the same time, beaming and holding out both hands to this very tall man like she'd known him forever.

Ingrid had her hand on his shoulder when Darcy joined them. "Darcy, this is Aidan Renaudin."

He took Darcy's hand, or rather her fingers, and gave them a delicate wiggle. She looked at their interlocking fingers, smiling at the ridiculousness of it in spite of herself.

"Hello," he said in such a way that his voice reminded her of syrup, slow and rich.

"Aidan is a nephew of Henry's younger brother by marriage." Ingrid leaned in toward Aidan, like she was about to share a secret. "Truthfully, I think you bear a stronger resemblance to my Henry than your father."

Ingrid laughed behind her hand, but Aidan didn't seem to notice. His full gaze was on Darcy, a look that was simultaneously bold and warm, and it spoke of his utter confidence. Darcy didn't trust him at once. The handshake started it, but the way this Aidan person was giving her a head-to-toe appraisal clinched the deal.

"Ingrid tells me you're going to give me the grand tour." He smiled with all his teeth, a Cheshire cat effect that made Darcy want to check for remnants of the poppyseed muffin she'd eaten for breakfast in between her own. His were impossibly straight and white, another reason not to take him seriously.

"That's what I'm here for." Darcy tried to sound cheerful, but her voice betrayed her, cracking instead.

Ingrid gave Darcy a curious look. "I'll leave you two alone for a bit. Darcy, why don't you start with the grounds and the cabins? Henry decided to take a midmorning nap. He should be up by the time you're ready for the house."

Darcy groaned inwardly and started toward the first cabin. If he didn't ask too many questions, she might get back home by noon. "So Ingrid says you're from Madison. Why are you interested in something so far from home?"

Aidan stuck his hands in his trouser pockets, taking in the view of the lake. "My family is from Duluth, like Ingrid mentioned. I've been in Madison since college, though, and own a few commercial properties there. I'd like to split my time between here and there eventually." He paused. "What did you like about working here?"

She looked at him sharply, not prepared to answer questions about herself. "Oh, well, I really like Ingrid and Henry. They're great people to work for." Darcy opened the door to the first cabin. The two rooms, quaint and light-filled, glowed from the ample windows overlooking the water.

"How would you describe your role here?" Aidan continued while he peeked into the bedroom then walked to the window.

"My role? Ingrid pretty much left me in control—the cleaning, the bookings, arranging logistics for the bigger events. Everything." Wasn't he supposed to be asking questions about the property? Darcy hoped the annoyance didn't show on her face.

Aidan opened the closet and raised his eyebrows. "Cedar? Nice," he said, and closed the door again. He flipped the wall switch for the ceiling fan. "So your responsibilities were greater than hers overall? Did you do any of the financials?"

"Excuse me, but am I being interviewed?" Darcy asked. "I thought you wanted to look at the property. It seems you're just interested in my job here." She stood behind him, waiting.

He turned and gave her that cool appraisal again. "I'm sorry if I seem rude. It's just that this would be a new venture for me. My other properties are apartment housing. This is a bit, ah—different. If I seem too bold, it's because I really don't know what I should be asking."

She laughed then and her mood lightened. "Maybe I should apologize. I didn't mean to make you feel uncomfortable." Darcy walked out onto the porch again and waited for him to follow. "No, I didn't take care of the books. I just accepted payments from clients when necessary for the large events."

They walked past the birch pergola and Ingrid's moon

garden, which fascinated Aidan. Darcy showed him the mounded artemisia, the four-o'clocks, and yarrow, and her personal favorite—the fragrant spindles of Russian sage, all of which seemed to glow when the moon lit the expansive lawn, Darcy explained to him. Ingrid's green thumb even coaxed the low-growing snow-in-summer to follow the flagstone path all the way to the beach.

"Where does that go?" asked Aidan, pointing to the path that led into a stand of white cedar.

"It's a path to a wild patch of blueberries a short way through there. It's very popular with the guests who stay, though I only tell the ones I like." As soon as she said it, she regretted it.

Aidan glanced at her, a wry smile twisting his mouth. "You just told me."

"No. Yes, I mean, of course I told you because you asked." Darcy turned away so he couldn't see her face turn red. Just shut up and he won't get the wrong idea.

"So you already have another job lined up?"

Darcy swallowed to make sure her voice behaved. "I'll be leading tours for a company in town starting tomorrow."

"Sturgeon Widows Tours." He rolled the name off his tongue like it amused him.

"They have some interesting stops. It's a great company."

Aidan stopped and looked back at the house. "This place, though. There's so much history here."

Darcy felt that he was trying to undermine her excitement. That and quizzing her about her job description at Blueberry Point Lodge suddenly put a bad taste in her mouth. She studied his profile as he inspected the house from where they stood. She couldn't help but notice how long his lashes were, the aquiline nose, though his self-assurance was a large part of his allure too. Was he even older than twenty-five?

"Should we go take a look inside now?" he asked, and he was on his way before Darcy could answer.

After another hour of touring the house, exploring each of the fifteen rooms, all the closets and nooks that old houses are known for, the third-floor ballroom, and down to the depths of the basement, where he inspected the jigsaw of copper pipes and the state-of-the-art boiler ("I'm the son of an HVAC guy. I know my mechanicals"). By the time Darcy finished with Aidan and they'd circled back to the French doors near the back patio, Ingrid rejoined them.

Aidan turned to Darcy. "Thanks for giving me time on your day off." This time when he shook her hand, he took it in both of his and held it. Those black-lashed eyes didn't give her a cool appraisal this time. Instead, his gaze was measured and encompassing. "Do you mind a call if I have other questions?"

"Not at all." His eyes were a most mesmerizing shade of gray, like liquid velvet.

He looked down at his feet in feigned modesty, but his smile suggested he knew the effect he had on her. Or thought he had on her. "You'll make a fantastic tour host. Good luck tomorrow," he said.

"Thank you." She slipped her hand out of his grasp before she started liking it too much. She hoped this was the last she saw of Aidan Renaudin. If he somehow managed to buy Blueberry Point Lodge, Darcy knew the place would change, and not for the better. For a reason she couldn't name, Darcy didn't trust him.

If only she had money—*lots* of it—the place could be hers.

Chapter Seven

❧❦❧

"So are you from Hendricks? Originally, I mean?"

The woman, sitting in the first seat behind Sean, had been peppering him with questions for the last ten minutes. Her complaints about the cold temperatures despite the bus heater blasting warm currents of air from the overhead vents were getting to him. That was the problem with early morning tours on the North Shore—no matter what the daytime temperature rose to, before noon meant extra layers. People from anywhere south of the Twin Cities didn't get it. To them, summer meant shorts and T-shirts.

Sean tore his gaze away from the front door of the tour building to look at her. "Yep. Born and raised."

"It's so isolated," she said, leaning forward now that she had his attention. "It's beautiful, don't get me wrong, but how do you get...things?"

"Things?" Sean glanced in his overhead mirror at the woman.

"You know, stuff. Do you do all your shopping in town? I mean, there's the grocery store, but what about household things—towels, furniture, a lawn mower—that you don't have to spend an arm and a leg for?"

Sean smiled. The question had a hundred variations, but it was the most common. Visitors to Hendricks marveled at the postcard scenery, shopped in the art galleries, and dined at restaurants like Red's Tavern or the seasonal Sego's, open only from April through October. Of course they wanted to move there. When the snow melted and the sun shone, when there wasn't a negative 40-degree windchill barreling down High Street off the lake, it was heaven. They might even pick up a Hendricks County real estate guide to check out what was available. But when they asked about logistics —how did you stock up for winter when you could be snowed in for weeks? Where's the best place to service your car? Exactly how much snow do you get? An annual average of 68 inches?—things got real. The questions stopped.

"Duluth is an hour and a half away. They have anything you need that you can't get here. Just takes a little planning."

He stared at his hands hanging over the top of the steering wheel and willed the woman to stop with her questions. He wanted to drive and not talk, didn't have the mental energy for it today. It was the first tour with Darcy Conti, the woman his mom hired, and Sean felt anxious. He always did when his routine changed. Would she fit in? Would their guests respond to her? He prayed she would so the company would have at least two people able to give tours since Melina was clearly not suited for any role outside of her office.

"I'll be right back," Sean said. Unbuckling the seat belt, he headed outside for relief from the relentless curiosity. And for fresh air. Those questions were suffocating.

Moments later Darcy came out of the lobby door, wearing a crimson coat, and Sean forgot about the woman and her annoying questions. The few guests who still milled about the patio immediately took notice. Darcy said something over her shoulder to one of them, those glossy curls brushing her shoulders, then the whole group followed her toward the bus like she was their homing beacon. A good sign. They were drawn to her. When she saw him, she smiled, the skin around her eyes crinkling. Sean rubbed his neck and returned her smile. He also silently cursed his mother's hiring tactics. If it wasn't against the law, Sean bet Emily wouldn't be above asking for a physical description and headshot for applications. This time she might have found the prettiest female in the entire Great Lakes region.

"Good morning," Darcy said, touching his arm. When she leaned close to him, that heady mixture of rosemary and cinnamon awakened his senses. "I've been studying all weekend," she said. "Hopefully I don't embarrass you too much. I'd hate to force you into taking over another tour," she whispered. "There's been enough of that, right?"

"You'll be fine," he said simply because, frankly, anything more involved would have required an awkward intake of air.

Sean waited for the last passenger to board before he climbed the steps, settled into his seat, and closed the door. As they rolled onto Main Street, Darcy's voice overtook the bus as she spoke into the microphone.

"Good morning! We're are so happy to have you aboard —" she looked over her shoulder at Sean's back—"Clem, is it?"

Sean nodded, smiling. She caught on fast.

Darcy went on. "Yes, it's true. We name our buses here at Sturgeon Widows Tours. You're riding Clem today. His brother, Clyde, is taking the day off." Laughter rose.

She cleared her throat and went on: "Here's a little background on the company before we make our first stop in about ten minutes. We've been in operation for twenty-four years, and run about three hundred tours each year. Our name is...a little unusual, yes?" She lowered her voice conspiratorially. "Basically the Sturgeon Widows was a women's social group back in the early 1900s. Since commercial fishing flourished in this area and men were often on the water for days at a time, sleeping in the large commercial vessels, their wives grew bored. These women planned progressive meals and card games—scandalous, I know!—visiting each other's homes for food and entertainment. The original Sturgeon Widows included twenty-five women when it first organized in 1903, made up of mostly Norwegian and Finnish settlers."

Sean listened to Darcy go on about the tour company. Her voice, lilting and rich, lulled him with its resonance. If guests complimented him regularly on his tour-giving skills, Darcy would soon be the favorite. He guessed Darcy could entertain them with a lively reading of his new log splitter's safety manual if necessary. Her command amazed him.

They headed northeast out of town, the last of the small lots with their clapboard Cape Cods giving way to the North Shore fauna of cedar, sumac, and birch. He slowed down to let a group of bikers cross the road in front of him as they made their way to the paved bike path running parallel to the highway. The group split, the faster riders bursting ahead of the slower ones once they hit the path. As the last of the riders rode over the highway and onto the gravel, Sean took his foot off the brake, still keeping an eye on the group. Their neon shirts bobbed together as he neared them on his right. They rode so close together.

Darcy continued. "Coming up on the left, if you see the bright red former schoolhouse and wonder why there is a metal sculpture of a beaver on its roof, well, I'm here to enlighten you."

The group's muffled snickers filled the bus, but they quickly turned to gasps as Sean braked in a hurry. He sensed Darcy gripping the seats on either side of the aisle to keep from pitching to the floor.

"What on earth—" she said as Sean pulled onto the shoulder.

He threw the bus into park and bolted from the driver's seat, lunging down the steps two at a time. The bikers circled back to one of their own. A woman was crumpled on the ground, clutching her leg as Sean jogged up to the group.

"Where do you hurt?" Sean asked as he knelt beside her.

The other bikers stood over them except for a teenaged boy. Next to Sean, he knelt beside her.

"Mom? Are you okay? Your leg doesn't look so great," he said. His voice wavered as he got out his cell phone.

Sean saw that her leggings were torn from her calf up to mid-thigh. A nasty abrasion left her shin and knee bloodied and covered with dirt and gravel dust.

"I'm fine, honey. Damn it," the woman said, sitting up. She undid the clip on her helmet and tossed it aside. "I don't think anything is broken." She checked her arms for injuries, and Sean saw more scrapes on her forearm and both palms. A quick glance around at her fellow bikers, she shook her head. "Sorry to start the morning out like this, guys."

Sean caught her arm when she tried to stand. She didn't appear to be disoriented, but he wondered if she might have other injuries. "Are you sure you're ready to get up? That was quite a wipeout."

Wobbly even as she clung to him, the woman sat back down. "Maybe not." She leaned against him, breathing hard.

Sean supported her back. He snapped his fingers and pointed at her water bottle, and one of the other bikers scrambled to unhook it from her bike. Sean unscrewed its cap and offered her the water. "Here, take a drink. Let's try again in a few minutes."

While the other bikers fussed over her, Sean updated his tour guests inside the bus. They'd be back on the road in no time, he assured them. Despite his Good Samaritan efforts, he'd be shocked if he didn't get a handful of refund requests because of this. This little distraction cut into the time they had paid for, and he couldn't blame them if they weren't happy with the tour experience at the end of the day.

"Thank you for stopping," the woman said to Sean when he came back, wincing as she slowly tested putting weight on her injured leg. She limped as Sean supported her, but within a few minutes was inspecting her bike, determined to double back into town and treat her cuts.

"Not a problem. But you definitely shouldn't ride," he said, thumbing toward the bus. "I have room for you."

The look of relief on her face was unmistakable when she saw the bus. "I think I'll take you up on that. As much as I like to think I'm invincible, I'm afraid my bike got the best of me today."

Her son said he'd wheel her bike back with his own, and meet her at their motel. Sean let the woman hang onto his arm as he walked her over to the bus. Darcy stood in the doorway, watching, her arms hugging her body.

"Sit with me while we take you back to town," Darcy offered. She helped the woman to the first seat as Sean got back into the driver's seat. "I'm so glad you're able to walk," she said.

Sean started up the bus and made a U-turn on the highway when the coast was clear. He wiped his neck with a bandana and tucked it back into his hip pocket while he listened to Darcy and the woman.

"Thanks so much for stopping, especially with a bus full of people," the woman said.

"Honestly, it looked more serious than it turned out. But he'd stop to catch a loose dog. He's like that."

The woman laughed. "Nice guy."

"Yes, he is. I'm Darcy, by the way."

"Hannah."

They talked until Sean pulled into the Flint Hills Motel and parked in front of her room. She thanked Darcy and Sean, saying goodbye, but Sean insisted on helping her to the door. As he boarded the bus again, Darcy moved to the seat directly behind his. He caught her eye in the overhead mirror, and her words echoed in his consciousness again, about being helpful. It was a curious thing to say on her part, especially when she and him hadn't started out on friendliest terms, and he might even make a liar out of her during the days to come. Yet her words kept playing on repeat in his head.

CONSIDERING THAT HELPING BIKE CRASH VICTIMS wasn't a part of the day's itinerary, Darcy was relieved when they were back on the road in record time after dropping off Hannah at her motel. The tour guests didn't seem upset by the sidetrack in their schedule. In fact, Darcy would bet that their end-of-tour evaluations would reflect the litany of praise she overheard from the rear of the bus while Sean helped Hannah to the door of her room.

"—didn't have to stop—"

"—he went above and beyond, didn't he?"

"—almost worth crashing for that kind of treatment."

Darcy apologized to the group for the delay, and since she'd already run through the dialogue for that part of the trip, she collapsed in the front seat and let the women talk amongst themselves while they waited on Sean.

Of course she couldn't help wanting to comment as he parked himself back in the driver's seat. He rubbed his neck like a knot of tension had taken up residence there, and she stopped herself before a sarcastic comment hovering on the tip of her tongue emerged.

"Impressive work, Superman." There. That was more sincere than snide.

Darcy looked at him in the overhead mirror. Except for a slight narrowing of his eyes and a quick glance at her reflection as he steered the bus back onto Highway 61, there was no reaction. Maybe he couldn't tell if she was being genuine or making fun of him. Darcy pressed her hand to her neck, trying to stop the heat from overcoming her face. Had her tone been off? *But I wasn't being glib. Really. Not this time.*

Minutes passed. With each second ticking away, her embarrassment grew. What upset her more? That he ignored her or that she couldn't help but make flippant comments even when she tried to compliment? Why couldn't she learn to filter herself?

"Thanks," he said finally.

Darcy thought she was hearing things until she looked up at the mirror. His eyes darted to hers and he lifted his eyebrows. When she didn't say anything, he shook his head slightly.

"What, you think I can't take a compliment?" he said over his shoulder.

"No, that's not it at all." Her mind raced. What was it then?

He kept his eyes on the road but asked in a low voice,

"And how would you know how nice I am anyway? We've met once."

"Truthfully? I have no clue if you're nice or not. But agreeing with a paying customer is good for business," she joked. When he didn't respond right away, she sighed. Why couldn't her sarcasm take a rest? "You seem nice. I mean, you did stop for her."

"I saw that crash coming. They were riding too close together."

"Do you bike?"

He shrugged. "Once in a while. I mostly hike and fish. You?"

"I love hiking. The trails here are fantastic. Rollie and I go every day after work."

"Rollie?"

"My dog."

"Which one is your favorite?" asked Sean as he turned into a gravel lot and parked.

"The Powder Rock Trail. It's closest to where I live." She shrugged on her jacket.

Sean pulled the lever to open the door. He turned sideways in his seat so he could look at Darcy. "So you probably live in the Mill Street Lofts?"

"Yes, for about a year now."

"Nice building. My brother helped renovate it."

"What's yours?"

He glanced at her. "My what?"

"Your favorite trail. Where do you like to go?"

"Oh. Definitely the Sage River Trail. Brandy likes that it runs right alongside the river."

"Brandy?"

"My retriever."

Darcy smiled. "I love big dogs. I have a corgi-shepherd mix right now, but my family has always owned big breeds. A Saint Bernard named Winston, an Irish wolfhound—Chief —super smart—"

Sean cleared his throat. "I hate to interrupt, but are you going to give the abbreviated version of the lighthouse spiel once we're outside or while they're still on the bus?"

Darcy looked out the window and saw the Clearwater Lighthouse right in front of her. She should have been talking about it well before they pulled into the parking lot. She threw her hands up. "Shoot!"

In front of her, Sean's wide shoulders shook with laughter. "Not a big deal. They have no idea that you're off cue," he whispered.

Wait—what? Off cue? She stiffened. He pointed out her simple mistake then laughed about it? Maybe she didn't want to talk to him after all. That wasn't her job anyway. She was supposed to be leading the tour.

Sean touched her arm as she turned to address the group. "Wait a sec."

Darcy drummed her fingers against the binder. "I'm already behind."

He took his hat off. "You're fine. I shouldn't have criticized you. I'm sorry."

His expression was so serious that a sarcastic quip didn't even come to mind. "It's all right."

He looked past her to the group, then lowered his voice.

"And, by the way, what you said to that Hannah woman was true."

She wracked her brain, wondering what he was talking about.

"You told her that I would have stopped the bus to catch a loose dog." He paused, watching her face. "You were right. I would do that."

Darcy laughed. "I could just tell that about you." She pulled the tour manual tight against her chest and looked away, embarrassed. Who was she kidding? She didn't know a thing about Sean Stetman other than he owned a tour company, fished every weekend, and was supposedly brokenhearted. Standing so near to him also strummed at her nerves—she knew that as well as her own reflection—and it was maddening.

Chapter Eight

S ean passed the old foundry building off High Street after leaving work two days later with Brandy in the passenger seat. He brought her to the office on occasion when he didn't want to leave her alone for the day. She was an ideal lobby dog: calm, friendly, and quiet. Even Emily, a stickler for a tidy, well-run office, loved having her there, keeping a stash of dog treats on top of the file cabinet.

He ran his fingers through his hair and the rooster's comb effect that he caught sight of in the mirror wasn't flattering, not that he cared. Still, he smoothed it down before noticing Matt's black truck sitting in the construction lot beyond the temporary orange fence that had been erected around the site. Several guys made their way out of the old factory, trudging over the newly churned dirt, lunch coolers in hand, swinging them into the beds of their own trucks. Sean spotted Matt as soon as his younger brother emerged from the building. He pulled to the side of the street and honked. Matt looked up and waved, then lumbered over.

Matt Stetman was a shorter, lighter version of his older brother. Much to Emily Stetman's dismay, Matt was also less focused, more impulsive, and too much of a spendthrift with what little money he earned. That is, when he worked long enough to earn a steady income. What he lacked in common sense and work ethic, though, Matt made up for with charisma. He was also a master carpenter, a talent he only halfheartedly put to use, even though he could have been booked year round if he had the gumption. Sean envied his brother's seemingly natural talent. Matt could frame a small building in half the time as him, even on a slow day.

"Hey, bro. Long time, no talk," Matt said as Sean rolled down his window. He reached across Sean to ruffle the fur on Brandy's neck when the dog tried clamoring over Sean's lap.

Sean looked over Matt's shoulder toward the building then back at his brother. "You've been busy. It's not because I haven't tried."

Matt scratched his cheek. "Yeah, sorry about that. I'm not the best at returning calls."

"No kidding. I've been leaving messages for what, five days?"

His brother opened his mouth to say something then seemed to think it a better idea if he didn't. Instead, he pressed his lips together.

"Could it have anything to do with reneging on our agreement to drive for me? I was counting on you."

Matt winced. "I'm really sorry. It was a jerk move." He hooked his thumb over his shoulder toward the foundry. "But when I got the call for this last week, though, I couldn't say no. This building—

Sean put up his hand. "I know, I know. It's exactly what you've been wanting to work on. I just...needed this."

"No offense, but you've been stewing for months. I'm no psychiatrist, but a bunch of alone time is exactly NOT what you need right now, in my uneducated opinion." He shrugged. "You're turning into a hermit."

"Funny." Sean settled back in his seat. If his intention was to make Matt feel guilty for not covering for him when he needed a break, it failed miserably. His brother refused to see he was blameworthy.

Matt tapped the side of his truck. "Hey, on the bright side, it sounds like Mom hired a worthy replacement. Word on the street is the new tour guide is a keeper." He raised his eyebrows.

"Too soon to judge. She just started this week."

"Sean, wake up. It's Darcy Conti. Don't pretend you don't know her. Every single guy in town knew who she was when she moved here last year."

"Sorry. Not everyone apparently. I must have missed the news bulletin." He did know who Darcy Conti was, in fact, but he wasn't about to say so. He'd never formally met her, so it wasn't a complete lie.

Matt threw back his head and laughed. "Only you would fail to see the opportunity here."

"How is hiring a new guide an opportunity?"

"Get a clue, bro."

"She's our employee, Matt. I'm not interested."

Matt tapped his index finger against his temple. "She's practically a genius, I hear. Did you know she went to SEMMI for deck officer training after she got out of the Coast Guard?"

"No, I did not," he said, though it surprised him. He hadn't seen her resume before Emily hired her. The SEMMI program was prestigious. He was impressed.

"Of course you didn't." He held up three more fingers, ticking off her other qualities. "Outdoorsy, pretty, single. And she can probably kick your butt."

"How do you know so much about her?"

"I just told you. She's not dating anyone. In a town this size every available guy is going to know all the details." Matt gave him a gentle nudge on the shoulder. "You're single, too, by the way."

"I'm aware of my relationship status, thanks."

Matt shook his head. "You are hopeless." He tapped the truck again. "Look, I gotta go. Beers tomorrow? Maybe?"

"Maybe. I've got things to do."

"Right." Matt gave him a long look. "The offer stands if you find yourself free any time soon. Call if you want."

"I'll keep that in mind." Sean returned the look until his brother left.

After he'd pulled back onto High Street, he drove up to the highway and stopped. A steady line of vehicles came from both directions on the single-lane highway, Hendricks's version of rush hour. He waited for a break and turned right toward home. He switched on the radio and flipped through a dozen stations before shutting it off, preferring the quiet. A half mile ahead, a brown sign alerted him to the pull off for the picnic area on the north side of the highway, a popular place for tourists passing through town. He couldn't remember the last time he'd stopped. Years, maybe.

The small lot was empty, save for a blue Honda with an orange tow notice on the windshield. He pulled next to it and shut off the engine. Straight ahead, the trail sign, nailed to a tilted post, pointed into the deepening shadows of the trees. He opened the door and Brandy bounded over his lap and out of the truck, clearly ready for some exercise.

"Okay, I get the hint," he said as he bent down to grab her leash. He led her over to the small pavilion next to the sign, and he studied the map covered in plexiglass of the two-mile loop of the Powder River Trail.

Maybe he needed to take more walks or meet Matt for beers or at least call his brother once in a while like he'd suggested. Maybe he needed to dive back into work, forget about brooding his life away. He'd wanted to develop a new tour stop or two anyway. Truthfully, the endless wallowing exhausted him. Sean just didn't know how to emerge from the funk he'd sunk into during the last few months.

Brandy pulled ahead, following the dirt path, nose to the ground. Sean stumbled along behind her, lost in thought, letting the rustle of leaves lull him with their whisperings. The path meandered up an easy but steady incline, and before long there was the sound of rushing water. Closer still was the distinctive padding of footfalls on the trail ahead. Then a bark.

When Sean looked up, Darcy was already standing still,

eyes wide, mouth slightly opened in surprise. Her dog tugged on the leash, straining to reach Brandy, who also wanted an introduction.

"Sean."

He really hadn't thought he'd see her. It was a crazy impulse to hike there, and after talking about their favorite trails just days ago, he wondered if she thought he was trying to run into her on purpose. Admittedly, that was what it looked like.

"I—I didn't expect to—" Even as he said the words, he didn't quite believe them enough to finish the thought.

She laughed. "See me? I didn't expect to see *you*. I thought your favorite trail was the Sage River one?" Tentatively, she eased Rollie closer to Brandy. They touched noses, and Brandy instantly bowed, rump in the air, her tail waving like a furry flyswatter. "Looks like Rollie doesn't mind sharing his favorite walking spot," she said.

"I was driving past and pulled in. It was pretty impulsive. I can't remember the last time I was here." It was the truth, but Sean was alarmed by his forthrightness. Warm and suddenly restless, Sean unzipped his jacket halfway. Every movement felt self-conscious and forced. What was his problem? Frustrated, he sighed loudly.

Darcy's brow knitted. "I didn't mean to interrupt your alone time. We're just heading back."

"No, no. You didn't interrupt." He came closer to better control Brandy, who was making quite the canine spectacle of herself in front of Rollie. When Darcy extended her hand, Brandy gave it an obligatory nudge then continued mingling with the other dog.

There was an awkward silence and a shuffling of feet. Their conversation stalled, Darcy looked as uncomfortable as he felt.

"Well, I'll see you tomorrow," she said, reeling Rollie in so she could get past them on the trail.

Brandy, however, had another idea. She lunged to get at Rollie, and suddenly the two dogs were wrapped around each other in a web of tangled legs and polypropylene rope.

"Rollie—stop!"

Darcy worked to unwind the leash from the dog's stubby legs while Sean tried to do the same with Brandy. Only Brandy, heavier by a good thirty pounds, bumped into him while he was already off balance, and sent him toppling over into a soft patch of foliage at the side of the path.

"Oh! Are you all right?" Darcy grabbed Brandy's leash as it trailed between them.

Sean propped himself up on his elbows. Embarrassed, he took Brandy's leash from her and looped it twice around his wrist.

Darcy offered him a hand. "I'm sorry. Rollie brings out the worst in other dogs."

His first reaction at seeing her extended hand was to take it. That he was probably double her size didn't occur to him until he tried getting to his feet. The effect was Darcy stumbling on an exposed rock in the trail as she struggled to pull him up. His hand slipped from her grasp yet momentum pushed her toward him, *over* him. In a blink, she somersaulted over his shoulder and landed on her back in the same patch of sarsaparilla, Rollie's leash still in hand.

The poor dog scrambled to her side, desperately licking her face like he was to blame.

Then she laughed, giggled like a kid actually, and it was so infectious, Sean laughed along with her.

"*That* was pathetic," she said.

"Remind me to think before I take your hand again."

Darcy rolled over on her stomach and rested on her elbows. "Wait, is this poison ivy?" She recoiled from the leaves that were inches from her face.

"No, just a little wild sarsaparilla." He squatted in front of her, careful to steady himself lest Brandy decide to take off.

She fingered the leaves. "Like the drink?"

"You don't want to drink anything made with that stuff." He extended his hand. "Need help?"

Darcy looked at him, at his hand, and smiled. "You like living dangerously, don't you?"

Her smile was nothing short of dazzling, Sean noted. Yet it was nothing compared to the jolt he felt when she grabbed his hand a second later, pulling herself to her feet. She noticed it too because she glanced at him and her smile faded, and they stood there a moment, a *long* moment, staring at each other, their hands growing moist in each other's grip.

He opened his mouth to joke about there being more to fear in the forest than him, but he thought better of it. Instead, he cleared his throat and said, "You did well today."

Her expression brightened. "Thanks. That means a lot coming from you. It's not like you give compliments every day, and—" Her eyes grew wider as she stumbled over her meaning. "I know you're not the best at—"

Sean put up his hand to stop her. "You're welcome," he said simply.

Darcy deflated. "Sorry. I ramble when I'm...nervous."

"Nervous? You?" Her revelation quieted his own tension for some reason.

Darcy shrugged. "I'm not 'on' all the time."

They looked at each other for an awkward moment. Her eyes dropped to Rollie's leash in her hands. She looped the handle around one wrist, then the other. Her shoulders rose as she took a deep breath. As Sean studied her, he wondered if he looked anxious too.

"Well, I'd better be going." She elbowed him playfully as she passed. "Enjoy your walk."

Sean watched her walk away into the lush canopy of the forest, her dark hair blending with the shadows. After a moment, her blue sweatshirt was like a tiny, bright bird bobbing through the trees. He glanced down at Brandy, who happened to be studying Sean like she couldn't bear to watch her human embarrass himself so. "I wasn't that much of an idiot, was I?"

Her feather-wisp of a tail swished against the ground.

Sean peered back down the trail, but no sign of Darcy remained. "I was afraid you'd think that."

DARCY KICKED OFF HER BOOTS ON THE MAT INSIDE her door, then unhooked Rollie's leash. The dog beelined for his bowl. Mad lapping and volumes of water splashing onto the kitchen tile didn't detract Darcy's overwhelming need to lay down though, as she collapsed on her bed. Maybe Bethany's constant needling for her to take up yoga had some merit. Aside from a brisk hike, what else did Darcy do to relax?

As if fate had read her thoughts and decided to insert a "think again" moment just then, a perfunctory knock at the door startled Darcy out of her brief respite.

"Darcy? It's me."

She hadn't made it off the bed yet before she heard the familiar voice—Mom. Seconds later, Darcy opened the door.

"I tried calling to you when you got out of your car, but you disappeared inside so fast." Fran Conti gave her a once-over. "You look like you just woke up."

Darcy opened the door wider so her mother could come into the apartment. "Thanks. It's been an exhausting day is all." She tilted her cheek toward her mother.

After Fran shifted the armload, she kissed Darcy. "I brought you some food," Fran said, shuffling the two bags again. She crossed the room to set them onto the counter. Then she opened the refrigerator door, shucking off her coat in the process. Darcy noticed her mother had traded her customary embroidered tunics and leggings for a hooded sweatshirt and yoga pants. She'd lost weight, too, and looked years younger than she was. Again, Darcy made a mental note to get into Bethany's studio. No excuses.

Rollie trotted over for an obligatory sniff, decided all was right with the world, then crossed the room to settle into his usual spot: the cushioned window seat overlooking Mill Street, and beyond that, the lake.

"Thank you. You didn't have to." Darcy pulled two plates, a bowl, and a juice glass out of the rinse basket in her sink and stacked them into their rightful places in the overheard cabinet before her mother commented.

"Really? I think I do." Wrinkling her nose, she held up a takeout container from The Silver Scale with Darcy's leftover cod from the night before. "Goodness knows you don't keep anything in here. How often do you eat out?"

"Hardly ever." Darcy opened her microwave, found her coffee from the morning, and punched in some numbers to reheat it.

Her mother offered a one-armed hug. "Oh, for heaven's sake, Darcy. No wonder you're tired."

Darcy faced her. "Mom, it's not every day. I told you I started a new job."

Fran held up her hands in mock surrender. "I'd forgotten. Sorry. How's it going?"

"I think I'll like it once I get settled." She plucked her coffee from the microwave, took a sip. "Do you want some tea?"

"No, thank you. So is this a transition job too?"

"What do you mean?"

"I mean, are you still considering graduate school?"

Darcy chewed on her lower lip to measure her reply. She'd never had trouble restraining her responses to her mother's questions. Maybe Fran intimidated her with her own unfiltered opinions, or she considered her mother's fragile frame of mind since her husband died. Either way, Darcy took care to think before she opened her mouth.

"I'm not opposed to it. It just doesn't seem like the right

time. I'm enjoying working for once on something other than schoolwork."

"You're giving bus tours now, right?" Her mother said "bus tours" as if it were a job that would leave Darcy morally wrecked.

Darcy lifted her chin defensively. "In a sense, yes. They're heavy on the regional history." She ran her finger along the rim of her mug. "You'd enjoy it. You should come on one."

Fran Conti's eyebrows arched in feigned excitement, but Darcy knew better. Once Darcy committed to joining the Coast Guard, her mother had made no effort to hide her joy that Darcy chose to follow in her father's military service footsteps. But that's where Darcy's interests separated from those of her father's. While he made the navy his career at Great Lakes Training Center near Chicago, Darcy found her passion in ships, *old* ones. Her first love had been the sleek cutters, like the *Polar Realm*, that she'd served on during her years of active duty, and the smaller but no less mighty ice-breaking tugs, which were used on the Great Lakes.

But once she'd finished with the Coast Guard, she enrolled in Southeastern Michigan Maritime Institute for deck officer training while also getting her two undergraduate degrees. There her fascination with state-of-the-art military boats evolved into an appreciation of the old relics that still lay beneath the cold, dark waters of the freshwater lakes, particularly along the same shorelines where she now found herself traveling near with Sturgeon Widows Tours. What she'd do with undergraduate degrees in history and anthropology was anyone's guess, but pursuing a graduate degree would at least involve research opportunities and from there, maybe a job with the National Park Service or independent projects with the Sea Research Board in Miami, Florida. Graduate school, however, would involve moving to the East Coast, the Carolinas or Maryland perhaps, where the most prestigious programs were located. And, well, she wanted to stay put. After the constant travel with the Coast Guard, she was ready to anchor down for the foreseeable future.

"Maybe I'll join you on a tour," Fran said, studying Darcy. Then her shoulders drooped. "I'm sorry. I came up here for a visit, and I'm nagging. I hate when I do this, really I do."

Darcy reached for her mom and hugged her. "I know. With Bradley gone all the time, there's no one for you to pick on now. Feel free. I won't hold it against you."

Fran smiled and took a seat on one of the stools. "Your brother broke curfew last weekend. I've had my fill of scolding for a while." She paused. "So Ingrid is for sure going to sell Blueberry Point Lodge? It's too bad. Such a lovely place for weddings and such. Maybe someone will take over."

"I think that's what she's hoping. In fact there's someone who came to look at it over the weekend. I had to show it to him. I think he's coming back when I help Ingrid with the retirement party in two weeks."

"Too bad you couldn't take it over." Fran looked pointedly at her.

Darcy shrank away from the idea. "I don't know the first thing about running a place like that."

"What do you mean? Hasn't that been your job for the last year?"

"Well, yes, but owning it is different. *Much* different."

Fran waved off the idea. "I'm sorry, but I don't see the difference."

Darcy drained her mug and set it on the counter. "And of course, there's the money thing."

"There's always money."

"*My* money, Mom. Remember that conversation last month about being almost thirty and earning my own living?" Darcy left out the other part of their discussion, namely her perpetual lack of a boyfriend.

Fran looked out the window, her lips pursing.

"And how could I earn my own living by going back to school, for that matter?" Darcy said it lightly, though it was a serious question. She resented being thought of as irresponsible. If anything, Darcy had always worked for what she wanted and worked *hard*—for money, grades, and especially in the male-centric Guard, respect. She realized all that toiling had left little room for personal relationships, especially dating, but her mother didn't understand that part. It wasn't that she didn't want to find someone special, but after making dating such a low priority for years, she'd never learned to take those initial steps to let someone know she was interested—the art of small talk, the flirting, the subtle nuances of revealing herself to someone during the course of weeks and months, instead of shouting "Let's start dating!" and expecting a positive outcome. Darcy smiled to herself at the thought. If only it were that easy.

"Maybe I could buy it as an investment and you could run it?"

Darcy laughed. "Oh, Mother! Be realistic."

"What? I'm serious." She leaned toward Darcy conspiratorially. "Think of it—you'd have total control without the financial burden."

"Just—no," Darcy said. She took her mother's hand. "I need to do this on my own. You understand that, don't you?"

Her mother's expression said everything that she didn't want to articulate to her daughter. Darcy knew her mother was lonely, Bradley in the house notwithstanding. She wanted an excuse to be closer to Darcy, and a business venture would be the perfect vehicle for that. If only Darcy felt confident that her mother wasn't doing it because she didn't have faith in her daughter. Fran Conti and the word "controlling" were mostly synonymous.

Darcy washed her mug in the sink then turned to face her mother. "Besides, I'm not even sure this is home yet."

Fran's eyebrows knitted together. "If you're not going for your master's and you're not calling this home yet, where else would you go?"

Darcy shrugged. "I'm just keeping my options open for now. I'm happy living in the moment."

Her mother let out a not-so-subtle sigh. "This sounds a little too free-spirited for you. You're speaking to a product of the sixties, remember. Are you sure everything's okay?"

"Yes, I'm positive."

Darcy turned away so Fran wouldn't see the deep scowl that settled on her face then. Even at twenty-eight, Darcy wasn't as positive as she liked to sound about her life's direction. After losing her job with Ingrid and Henry, and her uncertainty surrounding Sturgeon Widows Tours, everything seemed intertwined, off-kilter. Still, she caught herself grinning in spite of herself, remembering the tangled encounter with Sean and the dogs an hour ago. Awkward, funny, surprising—that was how she'd describe it to Bethany when she saw her friend next. Darcy bet the first words out of Bethany's mouth would be to ask for her impression of Sean Stetman. She could still feel the electricity coursing through his touch when he gripped her hand; there was no denying it. Darcy shook her head at the thought. No, she wouldn't muddle everything by dwelling on something like that. It could only complicate her life.

Chapter Nine

When Darcy walked into the lobby the following Monday, she found Melina and Sean huddled together over a book on the front counter. A momentary twinge fluttered somewhere in the vicinity of her lower rib cage, and she touched the spot hoping to rub it away. The curious sensation must have registered on her face, too, because Melina looked up and frowned.

"What's wrong?" she asked.

Darcy waved the question away. "Nothing." It wasn't necessarily the truth, but she couldn't name the feeling that gripped her suddenly and was gone.

While Darcy's dismissive comment seemed to satisfy Melina, since she returned to pouring over whatever had been keeping their heads together, Sean came from behind the counter.

"Sure about that?" he asked.

His face, ruddy from sun exposure during a weekend probably spent fishing, was even more impossibly handsome than when Darcy had last seen him three days ago. She could hardly look away from his eyes, which held her as if she were the only person there.

"Positive. Just thinking what I need to do before the tour."

She stuffed her hands in her jacket pocket and glanced around, trying to find something else in the lobby as a distraction from the man in front of her. The day's tour schedule lay on the desk behind the counter. She reached over the counter for it and studied the order of stops even though she'd memorized the agenda over the weekend. She shouldn't have arrived so early. It was a full hour before guests were due to board the bus. Darcy guessed she could stuff the guest folders instead of doing it after the tour. The lack of space at the counter, especially with Melina and Sean hovering, was a problem though.

As if reading her mind, Sean cleared his throat. "I have something for you."

She looked up. "Oh?"

He hooked his finger at her to follow him into the room next to his office, one she knew was no bigger than a glorified closet.

"I thought you could use this now that you're... official," he said, leaning against the doorframe. "It beats setting up shop in a two-by-two-foot space at the counter, right?" He reached across the doorframe to flip the switch on the wall just as she crossed the threshold. His arm stopped her.

"Sorry," he said, looking down at her, his eyes burning into hers. "What do you think?"

She lingered against his arm for a second or two longer than was necessary, and a familiar warmth spread across her neck and toward her cheeks. She tore her gaze away from his and peered into the room.

When she'd looked inside the room last week, stacked cardboard boxes, metal shelving, and plastic tubs of Christmas decorations filled the space. A worn artificial tree, its lights dangling to the floor, had stood forlornly in the corner. It was a sad, nondescript room. But now the metal shelving was gone. The cardboard boxes, tree, and decorations—nowhere in sight. Instead, a desk and an apple-green metal filing cabinet filled half the room. Framed photos of the lake and shoreline hung on the freshly painted gray walls. A computer monitor, printer, and phone took up space on the desk. Darcy realized she'd been holding her breath, but let it out when she noticed the vase of sunflowers, hot pink dahlias, and zinnias on the table opposite the desk.

"You didn't get the official welcome last week because, well, there were distractions," he said, emphasizing the latter part of his statement. "We're glad to have you here."

"This is fantastic—thank you. When did you have time to do this?"

"He was here all day Saturday," Melina chimed in. "I came in trying to get stuff done since Friday was a wash, and I couldn't concentrate with all the shuffling of furniture and paint cans."

Sean glanced at Melina, then looked again at Darcy. "I can move things around if you'd rather have the desk on the opposite wall."

Darcy laughed. "Not necessary. The arrangement, the *flowers*, everything is perfect." She placed her hand on his arm. "Perfect," she repeated.

Melina cleared her throat. "I hate to interrupt, but we have things to do before guests arrive." Her flat tone spoke volumes.

"I thought you said you were all caught up this morning?" Sean asked.

Speechless, Melina threw her arms up. She mumbled something under her breath before she sat down.

Darcy gritted her teeth when Sean caught her eye. Since her first day at the company, Darcy felt that Melina saw her as competition. She'd never said so, but Darcy knew Melina watched her every interaction with Sean for a hint of something more than a business relationship. Melina liked Sean. She'd said so herself. But Darcy didn't need the workplace drama, and she'd be damned if she'd let Melina try to intimidate her only because Sean arranged for Darcy to have her own space. There were greater concerns, namely that day's tour and the fact that Sean had not taken his eyes off her since he'd presented the office. No wonder Melina felt territorial.

After two hours of stops along Highway 61, Sean drove Clyde into the parking lot at Handmakery Folk Art School. The guests that morning were fiber artists from Duluth, up visiting the area for a day trip. One of Darcy's first tasks on the job last week was to confirm today's tour stop for lunch. Co-owner Letta Arbuckle, herself a national award-winning fiber artist as she so proudly stated to Darcy on the phone, was outside as the group pulled up. The bright and cloudless day seemed dull in comparison to Letta, whose ankle-length skirt might have held every hue of red, orange, and yellow. It stretched across her ample hips.

"It's so nice to meet you," said Letta after Darcy introduced herself. Hers was a meaty handshake. And noisy. A collection of thin metal bangles rattled together like castanets. "I was wondering when Emily would hire someone else so those two boorish boys of hers would stop scaring away her guests." She winked at Sean, who still sat inside the bus. He pointed to her with a mock warning.

Letta gave directions to the women as they exited the bus. They went inside the building, a rustic two-story cabin structure, while Letta continued on.

"So the plan is to feed them—we have a wonderful caterer in town who gives us a special price for these events —then give them a short tour of the place," she said. "Since this is your first time here, would you like to sit in with us?"

Darcy looked over her shoulder to see Sean walking across the parking lot to a small landscaped pond. A picnic table and mounds of perennial flowers and grasses surrounded the area, and two quaking aspens lent a little shade to the quaint spot.

"It's so nice out. I'll think I'll eat out here and keep him in line." She thumbed over her shoulder toward Sean. "But thank you."

Letta squinted as she looked past Darcy to Sean. "I could think of worse things," she quipped. Letta squeezed Darcy's shoulder, giving her a broad, knowing smile. "Enjoy yourself."

Was she implying they were...together? "Oh, we're not...I'm not..."

Letta put her hand up. "You don't need to explain," she said, laughing. "We'll be finished by one thirty."

Darcy grabbed her lunch box from inside the bus and crossed the parking lot. Why would Letta have that impression? Was she giving off some sort of vibe around Sean? Was he, and Darcy hadn't caught it? She stewed about this as she crossed the lot, absentmindedly kicking a rock until it rolled into the grass.

Sean lay stretched out on one of the benches at the picnic table. He'd flung his arm over his face to shield it from the sun and didn't know she was there until her lunch bag landed on the surface with a *thunk*. He flinched and sat up.

"Are you working on your tan?"

He rubbed his face. "Didn't sleep well last night."

She froze before she sat down. "Oh, I'm sorry! I can go inside and join—"

"No, no. You're fine," he said hurriedly. "If I nap now, I'll probably have the same problem tonight."

"If you're sure..."

He nodded and rested his elbows on the table as she sat.

Darcy unzipped her lunch bag. "Where's your lunch?"

"On the bus," he said, still watching her intently.

She laughed nervously. "Well, maybe you should get it. I won't be able to eat with an audience."

"You don't strike me as the self-conscious type."

Darcy unwrapped her sandwich. "No? What type am I?" She instantly regretted the personal question.

He studied her for a moment, his lips pressing together as he seemed to carefully weigh his answer. "Confident. Determined. Smart."

She nodded at his assessment. "I like those words."

"So you were in the Coast Guard." It was a statement, not a question. He'd done his homework.

"Yes. Loved it." She took a bite of her sandwich. "But after four years, I was ready for other things."

"Like SEMMI."

Now it was her turn to study him. "Have you been snooping, Mr. Stetman?"

He scratched at his beard. "We hired you, remember? You submitted a resume." He smiled as he said it.

"Uh-huh." She chewed slowly, enjoying the fact that he was almost squirming under her scrutiny. "What else do you want to tell me about myself?"

He laughed outright, a deep, resonant sound that shook his shoulders. "That's all I've got."

Darcy crumpled her plastic baggie. "I doubt that."

He turned away, a hint of a smile playing on his lips. Then he looked back at her. "How many pushups can you do in a minute? That wasn't on your resume."

"In a minute? Twenty-three when I first joined. Now it's probably under fifteen."

He nodded with the same unwavering look that made the hair prickle on the back of her neck. "Sit-ups?"

"Then? Thirty-eight. Now, maybe thirty, tops."

"I don't believe it. Let's see you."

She laughed. "Excuse me?"

"A challenge. I'll time you." He looked at his phone.

"If I'm going to get down in the grass and do sit-ups, you are too."

Sean blew air out of his cheeks. "I thought you'd say that." He took off his cap and smoothed the hair back from his forehead. The gesture was not lost on Darcy who had to tear her eyes away from the way his shirt buttons strained against the fabric. "I may need to train for that. I'll get back to you."

"Deal." She bit into her apple to keep from smiling and waited for the next question.

"How fast can you do a mile?"

"Back then my best time was 8:26. But I'm not a runner."

He drummed his fingers on the table. "Yeah, me neither. It always felt awkward to me, like I wasn't getting anywhere."

Darcy laughed. "Soo...your lunch. Aren't you going to eat?"

"Are we back to that?" Sean scanned the contents of her lunch bag. "Having an audience doesn't seem to be affecting your appetite after all."

She reacted with mock horror. "You distracted me."

"I run a tour company. It's my job to entertain and engage." He pushed up from the table. "Fine. I'll get my lunch if that's the only way you can stand to sit here with me. I don't want to scare you away."

"You flatter yourself. The only reason I want you to get your lunch is so that I can eat mine in peace," she said around a mouthful of apple. "Without all the agility questions."

He gave her a one-sided grin over his shoulder that made swallowing difficult as he headed toward the bus.

Darcy coughed to clear her throat. She gazed across the highway to the lake, which undulated like liquid crystal. The job wasn't going to work out if she kept looking at him as if he were someone other than her employer. Someone with whom she might want to walk dogs with or eat at Sego's or Red's together on a Friday night or walk on the beach when the moon was full. It was foolish thinking; she didn't need the distraction or risk losing her job. She'd just have to double down on her effort to suppress her—what? Crush? That was ridiculous. *Focus, Darcy.* His family employed her, his family employed her, his family—

"Do you like it so far—the work?" He was back, setting a red cooler down on the table. He swung one leg over the bench, then the other and sat down. "Answer honestly. Pretend it's not your boss who's asking."

Darcy stuffed the core into the empty baggie. "Yes, I do. I enjoyed it when I worked for Ingrid, though it was a little different. Meeting new people. Making sure they're having a good time. *Entertained and engaged,*" she said, throwing his own words back at him.

"It's too bad that Henry can't help keep the place up. They both love it there. My family owned it at one point way back when." He unwrapped his own sandwich and took two quick bites.

"You're kidding."

He held up a finger until he could finish chewing. "No. After World War II, my great-grandfather bought it as a gift for his new bride, my great-grandmother Ruth. My mother was born there."

"I love that. How long did they own it?"

"My grandmother sold it when her husband passed away in the early nineties. The Callahans have owned it since then."

"I had to show it to someone two weeks ago, someone maybe wanting to buy it."

Sean leaned forward and his eyebrows drew together. "I didn't know they'd already put it on the market. Who is it?"

"Well, they haven't. This guy is somehow related to the Callahans. Word got out that they weren't booking dates anymore."

"Who is this person?" Sean asked again. He set his sandwich down.

"His name is Aidan Renaudin. He said he owns apartment buildings in Madison but wants to split his time between there and here with a turnkey operation."

Sean threaded his fingers together and studied them. His mood was suddenly contemplative.

Darcy checked the time on her phone. "Letta is probably close to wrapping things up. We should check in."

"You're right. Are you ready for part two of the tour?" Sean pushed himself up from the table and stretched, causing Darcy to look away lest she linger too long on how his shirt pulled across his shoulders.

"*Semper paratus.*"

Sean looked at her quizzically. "What was that?

"Coast Guard motto. 'Always ready.'"

Sean gave her an intense look before a grin crinkled the skin at the corners of his eyes. "I'll keep that in mind."

Chapter Ten

✤❖✤

During the next several days, Darcy busied herself with organizing her office, and leading a tour each morning. Amid the busy schedule at Sturgeon Widows Tours and the number of hateful looks she deflected from Melina, her mind whirled with retirement party plans for the weekend. Notations in her calendar spilled onto loose sheets of paper, causing her to tape them into the burgeoning book. Saturday arrived with not enough hours to conquer Listaggedon. Finally admitting defeat, Darcy corralled Bethany into helping.

With four hands instead of two, the list shrank until Darcy felt confident she had party preparations under control by mid-afternoon. But a half hour before 150+ people were due at Blueberry Point Lodge for Henry's brother's retirement party, another problem presented itself in the form of a beagle.

"Where did he come from?" Bethany looked down at the

tricolored dog who wove itself around her legs as she and Darcy carried the last of the eight-foot folded tables across the lawn to the house.

Darcy glanced at the dog, trying to keep from slipping in the wet grass. "I have no idea. Be careful. He's really trying to get your attention, Beth." As if an overly zealous dog wasn't enough to deal with, a monster headache started to bloom between her eyebrows.

Bethany almost stumbled over him. "Buddy, you need to go away. I'm a cat person anyway."

That seemed to spur the dog on. He jumped on his hind legs, missing Bethany with his front paws. He tried again and Bethany turned to deflect his jump.

Darcy groaned. "Did you shower in beef broth this morning or something? Let's put this down for a minute. I need a better grip."

They lowered the table. Darcy flexed her fingers.

Bethany knelt beside the dog. Immediately, it lapped at her cheek until she held him at arm's length. "You get right to the point, don't you? Where'd you come from?"

"I think he lives across the highway. He's been here before. I think Ingrid feeds him too." Darcy shifted the table so she could grab it again. "C'mon. You can continue the lovefest after we get this table set up."

"Fine," Bethany said. She knuckled the dog lightly on his head before gripping the table again. "I'll bring you an hors d'oeuvre plate once everything is settled. Okay, baby?"

"I thought you're a cat person." Darcy felt the dog weaving through their legs again.

"He's cu—oh!" Bethany yowled and tumbled sideways

onto the ground. The table wobbled on its horizontal edge and fell away from Bethany onto the grass with a wet thud, narrowly missing the dog. Startled, the beagle let out a short yelp and took off toward the beach. Bethany grimaced, massaging her ankle.

Darcy dropped to her knees. "Are you okay?"

By the look on Bethany's face, it was a silly question. Darcy glanced toward the house. Ingrid was probably somewhere on the other side of the house, running in her own frantic circles.

Bethany eased off her sandal. "I think it's just twisted." She stuck out her hand. "Help me up," she said, though once standing, Bethany tested it. She grimaced and shook her head.

Darcy hugged her friend around the waist to bear most of the weight. "We're going to have to prop your foot up somewhere." The two made their way awkwardly toward the back patio.

"I'm sorry. I was supposed to be helping, not getting helped."

"Hey, it happens. No need to be sorry." Darcy strained to see around Bethany's hair that whipped against her face in the steady wind. "You do need to get your hair out of my eyes, though. I can't see where I'm going." Darcy could feel Bethany twisting to see something behind her. "Are you trying to make this hard for me?"

"Sorry! Just wondering who that is pulling into the drive in that incredible set of wheels."

Darcy didn't have to look to know it was Aidan

Renaudin. Unfortunately, she was expecting him. She groaned.

"Are you going to tell me who that is, or do I have to make a fool of myself to find out?"

"That's Aidan. He's here to get a feel for the place. He might be the new owner of Blueberry Point Lodge someday soon."

"Seriously?"

"I wish I wasn't."

"Why do you say that?"

Darcy shrugged. "The Callahans love it as a home. He wants it for a business venture." Darcy eased Bethany onto one of the stone benches and sat down too. They watched Aidan open his car door, grab his suit jacket from the backseat, and shrug it on with casual grace.

"He's so good-looking he's almost a walking cliche."

Darcy laughed a little too loudly, which caused Aidan to glance their way. He changed directions, walking toward them instead of the front door. Even from a distance, that overly confident smile spread across his face like warm butter and Darcy almost rolled her eyes. She hated herself for even thinking he was good-looking.

"He's too slick." She said it under her breath loud enough for Bethany to hear. "But you'll probably like him."

Bethany gasped in mock horror. "Are you implying I'm superficial?" She watched him approach, already beaming. "You know me so well," she said behind a toothy smile.

"Hello, ladies." He looked at Bethany and stuck out his hand before Darcy could introduce him. "We haven't met. Aidan Renaudin."

Bethany reached for his hand. "Bethany Marconi. Nice to meet you."

"Bethany just twisted her ankle as we were carrying that table." Darcy gestured to the table, which lay forlornly in the middle of the lawn. "She's helping...or rather she *was* helping me get ready for the party."

"Let me get you inside first, then I'll get the table. Do you mind?"

And before Bethany could protest, Aidan scooped her up in his arms like he was modeling for the cover of a romance novel. Watching Bethany's amused expression over his shoulder as she followed them into the living room, Darcy guessed Bethany would ask him for a date within the hour.

Since Bethany wasn't capable of doing anything but sitting, Darcy enlisted her to stay near the entrance and check people off the guest list as they began to arrive twenty minutes later. From there, Bethany directed guests to sign the guestbook then pointed them toward the double living room and atrium, decorated to honor Edward Callahan's 37-year career as a commercial airline pilot. That freed Darcy to keep the catering team in line—she should have known better than to try that new place in Dentsen—and answer Aidan's endless questions.

"What's the maximum capacity of these rooms?" Aidan stood against the wall near the piano, scanning the room like he already owned the place. He held a drink in his hand like a prop; Darcy had yet to see him take a sip.

She crossed her arms. "I'd have to look. Two hundred ten maybe?" That tall waiter with the blue-framed glasses was having trouble navigating the tight pockets of people. If

Darcy didn't stop watching him, she'd have a heart attack before long with the way his hors d'oeuvre tray kept tilting. She felt strangely at odds: wistful that it was the second-to-last event she'd host at Blueberry Point Lodge, yet relieved she wouldn't be babysitting caterers anymore.

Aidan grimaced. "That could be a problem."

"How so?"

"With the types of events I plan to use this space for, it's too small."

Darcy couldn't contain herself. "Too small? This place is almost 7,000 square feet."

Aidan's eyebrow arced. "Really?" He glanced around the room with its soaring ceiling and double staircase leading to the second of three floors. "Well, I guess I could open it up. Take down a few walls," he mumbled.

Darcy turned away from him so he couldn't see her frustration. He wanted to gut Blueberry Point Lodge? For the umpteenth time, she wished she had the funds to buy it from Ingrid and Henry.

He cleared his throat. "Maybe you're wondering why I'm interested in such an expensive property if only to bring in the sledgehammers and table saws?"

Darcy chewed on her lip, thinking about how to respond without hinting at her true feelings. If Ingrid was serious about selling the place to Aidan, she didn't want to jeopardize the deal.

"I hope I'm not interrupting."

The self-assured voice scrambled her thoughts and she turned around, startled to see Sean right there.

"What are you...the guest list...you're not..."

Sean chuckled. "No worries. I know I'm not on the official list. Ingrid asked me to come at the last minute."

Someone had cranked up the thermostat. That was the only way to explain why she suddenly wished she hadn't worn the lambswool cardigan over her sheath dress. Darcy pulled her hair away from the back of her neck to ward off the hot flash. The room was positively sweltering. Why didn't Ingrid tell her about adding Sean to the list?

She cleared her throat, but her voice cracked anyway. "Do you know Edward?"

Sean nodded. "Edward and Camille are my godparents. I wanted to personally congratulate them." Sean scanned the room, waved to someone near the buffet table, then settled his gaze on Aidan, who stood next to Darcy, silent and watchful. He stuck out his hand. "Sean Stetman."

Aidan squared his shoulders. "Aidan Renaudin. Pleasure."

Darcy still wasn't sure why Sean wasn't on the guest list if he knew Edward so well, yet was personally invited by Ingrid at the last minute. She was about to ask him when Aidan touched her elbow.

"Would you mind showing me the kitchen again? I don't remember much of the logistics from my first tour." He had yet to take his eyes off Sean.

Darcy sighed inwardly. "I'd be happy to." She turned her attention back to Sean. "The buffet table will be open soon. Bar's over there. I'll talk to you later?"

Sean smiled coolly. "Of course."

In the kitchen, Darcy leaned against a counter while Aidan inspected the space. She wanted to tell him that touring the kitchen while the catering company bustled about was a decidedly bad idea, but she was too tired to protest. Perhaps the less she said, the sooner he'd leave.

"You're dating…Sam?"

Darcy looked up at him. "I'm sorry?"

"That guy I just met. Are you two dating?"

Darcy straightened. "His name is Sean and no, we're not."

His eyes crinkled. "Good." He ran his hand over the granite island, oblivious to the white-shirted caterers—Benjamin and Greta—who shot him two equally irksome looks. "Have dinner with me tomorrow night?"

"I'm sorry. I have plans. Do you have any questions about the kitchen?"

He stopped caressing the counter top to look at her. "Can I have a rain check?"

"A rain check for questions?"

"No. For the date."

Darcy crossed her arms and looked pointedly at him. "I thought you wanted to look at the kitchen?"

He smiled a little too broadly. "I do, but that's not at the top of my agenda," he said.

Impatiently, she drummed her fingers against her biceps. "Look. I get that you want a date, but I'm not interested. This new job with the tour company is taking all of my energy. Now, I'm going to go rejoin the event that I'm hosting if you're finished in here."

He put his hands up as if to surrender. "Fair enough. I'm not used to not getting at least a first date. I won't ask again."

She swallowed her response that maybe he should be turned down more often, but the topic was closed from her point of view. Benjamin and Greta had left with full trays of food and had thankfully missed their tense exchange after Aidan asked for the date. She uncrossed her arms and looked at the space. "All of this talk about knocking down walls and such has me wondering how much you want to expand?"

He stuffed his hands in his pockets and perused the room. "With the lodge? I'm picturing a mini-resort. Totally revamping the inside here—making it all entertaining spaces by gutting the bedrooms—and tearing down the cabins to make room for a smaller version of the main building. Essentially, I'd love to have the largest resort on the North Shore."

Darcy gave a short laugh. "That's not saying much. There isn't another place like that between Duluth and the border."

He pulled back as he looked at her. "You don't sound like you like my plans."

She dropped her gaze to the floor, contemplating her response. She didn't want to tell him that she loved Blueberry Point Lodge just as it was. She didn't want to appear desperate, especially since he seemed to enjoy having the upper hand. "It's none of my business what you do here."

Aidan studied her for a few seconds before he got one last look at the kitchen. "Maybe we should rejoin the party."

She couldn't think of a better idea.

SEAN WAS TALKING WITH BETHANY WHEN DARCY and that Aidan person came from the kitchen. Darcy's pinched expression made her prettier than ever. She moved fluidly through the crowd, chatting with several of the guests and introducing Aidan to them, then whispering to a server as he walked back toward the kitchen with an empty tray. When Sean tore his gaze away from Darcy and looked down at Bethany, she grinned. Bethany sat on the edge of a couch with her twisted ankle propped up on a red corduroy ottoman. She patted the cushion next to her.

"No, thanks. I'll stand." He was too tense to sit. He didn't like seeing Aidan hovering near Darcy, and he most certainly didn't like crowds.

"Suit yourself," Bethany said. "By the way, you're about as easy to read as a marquee in Times Square."

"That's the first time I've been called easy to read. What do you mean?"

"You've fallen for the intelligent yet subtle charms of my friend, haven't you, young man?"

Sean exhaled deeply and shook his head. "Hardly. And let me remind you that I'm a year older than you."

Bethany chuckled. "Please. Get your head out of the water. You should spend less time fishing by yourself and more time hanging out with good people. One bad apple shouldn't ruin a person for life."

"If you're talking about...her—

"Yes. Paige. Let's just spear that elephant in the corner."

"Okay, *Paige*. She has nothing to do with anything."

"Good. Because Darcy is an amazing person."

Darcy left Aidan behind with a small group and was

making her way over to Sean and Bethany. He smiled as she approached, but said in a hushed tone to Bethany, "I don't doubt that."

"The party seems to be humming along smoothly. Well done," Bethany announced as Darcy stopped in front of them.

"Yes, you run a tight ship." The words had almost stuck in his throat. Talking to her seemed to do that to him lately.

"Ha! No pun intended, right?" Darcy looked down at Bethany. "How's your foot?"

Bethany poked at the skin around her ankle. "I'll live."

Sean lifted his chin in Aidan's direction. "So he's the one that wants to buy this place?"

Darcy sighed. "That's what he says." She held up her hand. "I'm sorry. I can't talk about him or my heart will start racing again."

Bethany lifted her glass and let an ice cube tumble into her mouth. She crushed it before saying, "I know what you mean."

Darcy shook her head at Bethany. "He's no good for you."

Waving her off, Bethany set her glass down. "He's good for one free meal, but that's about it. I'm not interested in any man who looks like he spends more time in front of the mirror than I do."

Sean met Darcy's amused expression with his own and their eyes locked before she looked away. The electrically charged exchange didn't escape Bethany's notice either. Again, Bethany nodded knowingly at Sean with a self-satisfied smirk.

"Can someone get me another refill from the buffet?" Bethany held her plate out. "All of this sitting around is making me hungry."

Sean took her plate, wanting the excuse to escape before Bethany put him on the spot with Darcy. Edward stood near the buffet anyway, and he hadn't congratulated him yet. "Be happy to," he said.

An hour later, after the alcohol-fueled speeches by Edward's coworkers and a brief, heated conversation with Aidan about how preserving the ecology of the beach near the house was more important than developing it for commercial purposes, Sean had enough. He shrugged on his coat and reached for the front doorknob when he felt a hand on his back.

"I'll walk you out."

It was Darcy.

She shut the door behind them, sealing the party banter and piano music off from the hushed surroundings outside. The lake, invisible yet always watchful in the distance, lapped against the shoreline. A soft, cool breeze ruffled Darcy's hair against her face.

"I'm glad you came. Sorry for giving you a hard time about not being on the guest list," she said, her voice as smooth as the velvet night.

"You sure know how to make someone feel welcome."

Her smile dulled the moonlight in comparison. "Now you're just rubbing it in."

"Never."

They walked over to his truck. He put his hand on the

handle, but didn't want to get in just yet. What did he want?

"You seemed to know almost everyone in the room," she said.

He looked at the house, lit up like the moon itself was confined within its walls. "The plus side of growing up in a small community."

"The Chicago suburbs definitely weren't like that. Families seem so transient near the cities, coming and going all the time. Nothing there is permanent."

"Permanent can be good."

Her eyes lingered on his. "I agree."

Several seconds of silence passed between them. Sean wanted the conversation to continue but was at a loss as to how to prolong it. Darcy, too, seemed uncharacteristically quiet. She stood before him, looking up into his face, her dark eyes shining like half-lit embers. Was her expression more buoyant than usual or was it only his imagination? He wasn't sure. He didn't know her that well.

His gaze travelled to her lips and lingered there, wondering what would happen if he suddenly leaned forward. Would she let him kiss her? Or would she step away? When she took a deep breath, he looked up at her again. Eyes wide, Darcy watched him, her mouth slightly opened.

"See you on Monday, I guess," she said. A hint of a smile curved one side of her mouth. Did she know what he was thinking?

He squeezed the door handle. It clicked, the inside light

popped on, bathing them in a stark, unwelcoming light. He slid onto his seat. The seat leather groaned.

She watched him get in, her arms hugging her body.

Sean hesitated, again studying her lips and the way they pressed together with that slightly amused grin.

"Yes, see you Monday," he answered before closing the door.

If he got through tomorrow without wishing the day away, he'd be surprised. Sean had never looked more forward to a Monday morning.

Chapter Eleven

❧❦❧

On Monday afternoon, Sean sat in the lobby, finishing a lunch meeting with Emily and Melina, after he and Darcy had given a morning tour. He looked at the clock. Darcy should be back any minute from lunch, and then he would ask her what had gone wrong.

The tour seemed to go smooth enough, he thought, but as soon as he'd pulled Clyde in front of the building at the tour's end, Darcy bounded off the bus. Surprised at her abruptness, Sean said goodbye to the guests and went to look for her. When he rounded the corner of the building, her Jeep pulled away from its usual parking space, the vehicle's signal blinking on as she turned onto Mill Street. Maybe she had errands to run.

So when Darcy appeared minutes later, a takeout box from North Shore Co-op's hot bar in hand and a dark look on her face, Sean stood up.

"Do you have a minute?"

Darcy stopped, looked from Melina and Emily, then at him. She nodded and walked into his office. He followed.

She sat down in the chair beside his desk, resting her forehead in her hand.

Sean eased himself into his own chair. "What's wrong?"

Silently, she studied her fingernails on her other hand. She shook her head.

"Was it something about the tour?"

She shook her head again, but then her shoulders dropped like the weight of whatever upset her was too heavy a load. "I don't know these places like you do. You talk about them like you love them. Like they're in your heart." She paused, and dropped her gaze to his flannel shirt, like she could see beneath the fabric into his chest and the source of this deep affection. "I just know them on paper. It's frustrating."

"What brought this on?"

She looked up at him. Her eyes flickered with an intensity not unlike a flame catching tinder. "They think I'm a fraud." She gestured toward the lobby.

"They? What are you talking about?" He reached for her, his fingers brushing hers before he thought better of it and retracted. Darcy's eyes widened. It seemed like a natural reaction, but it surprised Sean. He wasn't a touchy guy. "Sorry. Tell me what happened."

She slumped against the chair then and sighed heavily. "While we were at the lighthouse, a couple asked how long I'd lived in Hendricks."

Hesitantly, he said, "Okay." Sean couldn't see where this was going.

"I said to them a little more than a year. Then the man told me he could tell I hadn't been here long because I sounded like a talking brochure."

Sean understood her frustration. "There will be guests that are, frankly, asses. I'm sorry you met one this morning."

Darcy pressed her lips together with a look of stubborn resolute. "I am NOT a talking brochure. It was such a rude thing to say," she said, her voice rising.

"Like I said, you'll get one of those every once in a while. Don't let it get to you."

"I can't help it. It's my nature. I can be an obnoxious perfectionist."

He smiled at her. "Admitting it is the first step to recovery they say."

DARCY LEFT HIS OFFICE A FEW MINUTES LATER and walked to her own, sitting down in the plush rolling armchair. Had Sean just tried to hold her hand? By the look on his face, the gesture shocked him as well. She pressed a hand against her throat, feeling the warmth still flushing her skin.

She stared at her corkboard wall, installed over the weekend. It had been an afterthought on his part when she'd casually mentioned her dislike for Post-it notes. They lost their stickiness after a while and then she misplaced them. She liked bulletin boards, Darcy told him. Her rambling comments about Post-its registered with him apparently because when she'd come in that morning, she caught Sean in her office moving her furniture back in place. A four-by-four-foot section of cork decorated the wall behind her desk. As a final touch, he'd tacked a copy of a photo a guest had taken last week of Emily, Melina, Sean, and her. Darcy noted with a smile how Sean's head tilted toward her own, his hand on her shoulder.

While studying the photo, Darcy sensed a presence a few moments later. She startled when she looked up. Sean was there, leaning against her doorframe.

"Sorry. Didn't mean to scare you." He glanced at the lone photo decorating the space over her desk. "The bulletin board. It's still bare."

She settled back in her chair. "That's the least of my worries."

"Worries? What are you worried about?"

"That I'm not cut out for this."

"Don't take this the wrong way, but I think you're taking his comment too seriously."

She shook her head. "This is my job. I want to do well."

Sean studied her for long moment, seeming to carefully consider her words. Her face burned under the scrutiny. His eyes mesmerized her, the hazel irises fringed by a ring of gold, and she had to look away lest she fall into them.

Finally, he said, "Wednesday. Are you busy after work?"

"No," she said, though she knew her to-do list, sitting on the middle of her kitchen table, filled a full sheet of paper, front and back. The last event at Blueberry Point Lodge was in two weeks—the Osgood wedding. There was a mixture of excitement and dread since it was the last time she'd be involved with anything there. She'd be putting in several hours each night from now until that weekend.

"Then we have work to do," Sean said matter-of-factly, and something clouded his face. He didn't wait for her reaction. He didn't say another word. He simply walked out of his office, through the front door, and out onto the patio. Moments later, she heard his truck roar to life.

Darcy sat there for another minute, her heart drumming a different rhythm. What did "we have work to do" mean? His mercurial mood swing left her wondering what she'd said. Did he realize her sensitive nature might not be such a good fit for the company? Maybe he felt resigned to retrain her. Was this the first step toward losing her job? It couldn't be. Emily seemed happy to have her there and she had done the hiring. What power did Sean hold over her when his own mother demoted him and filled his position with her? And just minutes ago, he seemed to have sympathized with her when she mentioned the unruly guest, and the unmistakable charge they'd felt when he touched her hand. He was so hard to read.

Darcy would simply avoid talking with him about anything other than the tours. She needed this job. She'd double down on keeping their relationship strictly professional. No more joking around or sitting together while they ate lunch during the daylong tours. Maybe she'd even enhance some of their tour stops with a little more anecdotal history; a few of their stops' scripts needed some livening up. Yes, she'd start with the Sage River stop. A little research would keep her mind occupied and convince any doubtful tour guests in the future that she knew as much about Hendricks as any lifelong local.

That night, Darcy sat in the corner of the children's section of the J. Broman Library, reading wedding announcements in old issues of the Hendricks newspaper. It was quiet that time of night, an hour before closing, except for the two librarians at the circulation desk tossing books onto a rolling cart for restocking. Darcy startled when Bethany strode up behind her and crawled her fingers across Darcy's back.

"I found four names for you. My sources tell me these are bona fide couples who made proposals at the shelter at some point." Bethany floated a sheet of notebook paper onto the table in front of Darcy.

Darcy fingered the paper, noted the names and phone numbers written in purple ink, and nodded. "Good work, Sherlock."

Bethany pulled out a chair and sat, setting a floral canvas bag on the seat next to her. "Tell me again what the full spectrum of my investigative skills is being used for?"

Darcy tucked the hair behind her ears and sat back. "I'm expanding the tour stop there. I need some cute stories."

Bethany winced. "If my future husband took me to a mosquito breeding ground, which is exactly what the Sage River Trail is, to propose? Well, I'd tell him to bug off. Pun intended."

Darcy giggled. "Romantic gestures are a subjective topic, I guess."

She pointed to the newspaper in front of her. "Listen to this one: 'Kevin Kelley and Wendy Hildenbrand were engaged on Nov. 15, 1985, at the Sage River shelter. Kevin proposed to Wendy in the candlelit shelter after snowshoeing the Sage River Trail by moonlight. There he presented the ring, an heirloom diamond from his great-grandmother, the late Virginia Kelley, which had been reset recently by RJ Reed Fine Jewelers.'"

Bethany slumped. "Charming," she droned. "Never mind that it's Arctic-grade cold in November. You wouldn't have gotten me out of the car, diamond ring or not."

Darcy shook her head, smiling. "So anyway, I'm going to interview these people." Darcy tapped the paper Bethany gave her. "Some personal anecdotes will make the stop a little more interesting. Who can resist a good love story?"

"Me." Then Bethany perked up. "Speaking of romance, how do you like working with Mr. Perfect?"

Darcy pressed her lips together, refusing to look at Bethany. Now was not the time to acknowledge that Bethany had been right. Darcy found Sean Stetman every bit as good-looking as Bethany had gushed about. They had plenty in common too. Unfortunately, nothing would come of it, not with Darcy's new commitment to keeping business and pleasure separate.

"Don't tell me." Bethany snapped her fingers. "This 'research' is giving you ideas for when you propose to him. Tell me I'm right."

Darcy felt her heart thudding underneath her sweatshirt at the thought. "That's ridiculous."

"What, you don't like him?"

"It's not important. I'm an employee. He's the owner's son. End of story." Her finger followed the article as she tried to read, though she wasn't comprehending a single word. Frustrated, she blew air out of her cheeks and sat back.

Bethany squinted. "Uh-huh."

"Truth."

Bethany grabbed her bag. "Whatever makes you feel better. Just remember, when wedding bells are ringing for you two, I better get a thank you."

"And what exactly will I be thanking you for?"

"For being the one who called the relationship of the century." Bethany picked up the newspaper in front of Darcy and pretended to read: 'Darcy Conti, tour guide at Sturgeon Widows Tours, hooked company owner Sean Stetman into marrying her—'"

Darcy laughed in spite of herself and grabbed the paper back from Bethany. "You can go now."

She watched Bethany leave. A few minutes later, the librarian brought over a copy of another shelter proposal story after searching the library's database. Darcy thanked her. But suddenly her heart wasn't in it. She didn't want to think about other people's happy endings anymore that night. Darcy tucked the paper with names and numbers into her binder. Maybe she'd call one or two of them tomorrow during her lunch hour. Then she'd tell Emily about her plan to add some new anecdotes to the tour script. If she focused on rewriting a few of the stops, Sean's last words to her might stop repeating themselves in her head.

Chapter Twelve

✣

On Wednesday afternoon, after Melina and Emily had left early for the day, Sean popped his head into Darcy's office. He hooked his finger at her. "Let's go."

Darcy followed him outside with a knot of anxiety sprouting in her chest, wondering what he had planned. She was also angry, angry that she let herself get worked up about probably nothing. There was no indication from him or Emily that her job was in danger. She knew they desperately needed help, and she was experienced in hospitality, whether she was planning retirement parties and weddings or leading groups of tourists around the North Shore in those ridiculous fish-topped buses. In fact, the more she thought about it as they walked toward his truck, the more her anger swelled. She took a deep breath, trying to suppress the feeling lest she say something she'd regret.

He opened the passenger door for Darcy and walked contemplatively around the front of his truck before he got in.

She buckled her belt. "Where are we going?"

Sean had been especially quiet all morning on the tour. It had been a short one, just a quick drive ten miles west of town as far as the lighthouse, and then back through Hendricks to Dentsen. The group of eight women friends from St. Paul had signed up for a mixed media fiber arts workshop at Handmakery Folk Art School. Sean picked them up at three o'clock and dropped them off at the Flint Hills Motel.

"You'll see," Sean said, his eyes fixed on the road. "You don't like surprises?"

Darcy smiled, her heart lightening a little at the sound of his tone. "I do. It's just that...did I do something wrong?"

Sean slid his hand off the wheel and rested his arm on the seat back behind her. "No."

Darcy supposed she should have been content with that, but Sean seemed distracted anyway. She didn't know him well enough to know what triggered him. Something had happened in his office two days ago, and she'd yet to figure out what it was.

When they pulled into the gravel lot of Blueberry Point Lodge, she was as confused as ever. Sean shut off the engine and looked at her, the skin on the edges of his eyes creasing ever so slightly. He put his finger against her lips when she opened her mouth to speak. "Too many questions defeat the element of surprise." His amused expression was contagious. Darcy laughed and got out of the truck.

The late-afternoon sun shone on the September landscape, turning the golds and scarlets and umbers into even richer versions of themselves. On the clearest days, it was as if an artist had traced the landscape, every ridge of bark, blade of grass, and basalt cobble, with a graphite pencil, defining the already distinct edges. The lake, a cobalt shade reflecting the sky, stood still as if holding its breath. Sean dug behind his seat, and pulled out a vinyl tote. When he realized Darcy was watching him, he smiled and lifted the bag. "An early dinner."

"Really? Now I am surprised."

That same not quite smile lingered on his lips as he motioned for her to follow him across the lawn and onto the path through the cedar. Amongst the trees, Darcy pulled her coat tighter around her neck. The breeze lifted the hair off her face, and she burrowed into the folds of the coat. The path was too narrow for them to walk side by side, but Darcy was content to watch him ahead of her, his broad back made even more so by the sable canvas jacket. Cedar flags muffled their footsteps along the dirt trail, and soon the path gave way to the open patch of ground where the blueberry plants thrived. Their foliage, a deep russet red by now, quaked in the breeze.

Sean brushed past a patch of sumac and turned off the main path to follow an even more tapered trail through the bushes, one she had never noticed in all of the times she had led groups there for berry picking. As if sensing her curiosity, Sean announced over his shoulder, "Deer trail."

Darcy almost asked another question but decided against it. She didn't want to ruin his surprise. When they came to a stand of chokeberry, Sean held aside the branches, then passed her again on the path, regaining his lead. The foliage opened up as they neared the lake, but Darcy knew they were quite high from the beach itself, coming up to the rock outcrop with its sheer drop onto the rocks below. It was a twenty-foot span between ledge and ground, so if a person wasn't paying attention, the distance would come as a painful, and possibly deadly, surprise. She'd never stood at the ledge, having only then realized the trail led to it, so she followed Sean and trusted he knew where he was going.

"Sean?"

She'd lost sight of him. One minute he was ten feet in front of her, lumbering through the overgrowth, then he was gone. How could he disappear so quickly? Darcy stopped, straining to hear his footfalls or his movement through the bushes. Nothing.

"Sean?"

"Down here." His voice was muffled and considerably lower, like he was underground.

"Down where?" The vegetation was so thick she could see only ten feet in front of her. Darcy didn't want to move too fast for fear she'd walk off the ledge wherever it was.

"Follow the path."

She inched her way along the trail until it dipped between two boulders on either side. The farther she went, the larger they loomed until the narrow passage descended toward the beach. The path continued to weave and twist its way amongst the basalt walls until she stepped onto the cobbled beach, a clearing of sorts, yet the rock walls on either side extended their way to the water. The effect was a small, private cove. Darcy marveled at the area, a place she never knew existed, though she'd been down to the water dozens of times during her time at Blueberry Point Lodge.

"This is beautiful."

"That it is," he said, though he wasn't looking at anything but her. The bag he had been carrying was at his feet, a blanket spread underneath it.

"How did you know it was here?" She picked up a palm-sized granite cobble, examined its gray-and-pink clusters for a moment, then tossed it into the water.

"I had the canoe out one day and went past it. It's the prettiest spot on the whole North Shore, I think."

She walked over to the blanket and sat down, stretching out her legs. Within the wall of rock, the sun baked the area, chasing away any chill that normally would sprout goosebumps. Darcy peeled off her coat.

Sean stood there, looking down at her, seemingly at a loss for what to do. Darcy patted the ground beside her. She lay against the blanket and stretched her arms above her head. When he offered the water bottle to her, she propped herself up on one elbow and drank, a little stream of water running down the side of her chin and dampening the neck of her shirt. Then she handed back the bottle.

Sean kept his eyes on her as he screwed the lid back on the bottle.

"Are you going to sit down or stand there all day?" Her tone was off, more gruff than she intended, but he made her feel self-conscious.

He sat down, folding his knees up, arms encircling them. After a while, he shrugged his jacket off too. His body heat underneath the coat carried the scent of wood smoke and soap, and Darcy inhaled to capture its full essence.

She lay on her side after a while, propped up on an elbow, and stared at his profile. She found it curious that after all of this—packing the bag and hiking to the secluded spot—he seemed as flustered as a teen in the throes of his first crush. She regretted the analogy as soon as it popped into her head, and mentally pushed it away. She might have even grimaced.

At first glance, he seemed more interested in the lake than in her, but with careful observation, it wasn't true. His stiff posture belied the casual drumming of his fingers and the pulse point on his neck beating like a hummingbird's wings. She had to be careful not to say or do anything that might give him the wrong impression.

"So what 'work' are we doing here?" There had to be more to this rendezvous at the lake than dinner and chitchat.

Sean looked at her. "I'm sorry?"

"The other day in your office you said we have 'work to do.' I can be dense at times, but I don't see how this has anything to do with my retraining."

His forehead furrowed as he considered her words. Then he eyed the lake again. "You said you didn't know these places like I do."

"Yes."

"This is where it started for me."

It was her turn to be confused. "I don't understand."

"It's my home."

"What does that have to do with me being a better tour guide?"

"Do you love it here?"

"Of course."

"What do you love?"

Darcy looked out at the lake, a waterscape of jewel tones in constant motion as the sun dipped in the west. "I love the lake, the people, the community. It's just the right size, low-key, beautiful during every season of the year."

Sean smiled. "You love it for all the same reasons I do. And yeah, I grew up here, so my connections run deeper, but in time you'll make them too. And when you talk about this place, people will know that you love it, that it's home, even though you've only been here a short time."

Darcy surveyed their private beach. "So why are we here?"

"Because of all the people I know that grew up in Hendricks, no one but me knows this is here. And now you do." He raised his eyebrows at this revelation before he reclined, resting on his elbows.

Darcy didn't know what to say at first. The gesture stunned her into silence. That he shared it with her and only her seemed a rare privilege, and she knew for certain that moments like that in the life of Sean Stetman were few and far between. She swallowed, hoping her voice wouldn't betray her when she spoke.

"And I can now lead tours with utter confidence because I'm not just a talking brochure, but someone with insider knowledge," she said, her tone light.

Grinning, he said, "Exactly."

She kicked the pebbles at her feet, sending them skittering closer to the water. "I do love it here. In Hendricks. The pace suits me. I hated growing up near the city."

"A few weekend trips to the Twin Cities every year suits me just fine," Sean mused. "Can't imagine living anywhere else."

Darcy turned her head to mention that she did miss certain places, though, like the Art Institute—growing up she'd visit two or three times a year, good memories—and as she did, the breeze lifted a stray curl and it brushed his cheek. It startled him, and he shifted his weight away from her as one does when a fire rages too hot and the heat becomes unbearable. But then he caught himself, and when he gently tucked the errant strand behind her ear, Darcy's breath caught.

Their eyes locked. She searched his face for something—what? A signal? A hint he wanted the same thing in that moment—to feel a whisper of breath, the texture of lips.

He stretched out along side of her, still inches apart. The hush of water pushing against the shoreline, and the whistle of herring gulls lulled Darcy and numbed the feeling of the rocks beneath the blanket cutting into her hip. Tentatively, she reached for his face and traced a line from his jaw, the soft beard hair tickling her fingertip, to the corner of his mouth, and slowly she moved forward, and touched his lips with her own. It was decidedly not how she planned to keep her distance.

"I'm not sure—" Sean started to say, breathing the words against her mouth. He pulled away slightly, but then exhaled deeply as if giving in, and he slid his hand across her waist to her back, pulling her toward him.

Darcy's pulse quickened at the mixed signal. His body language was telling her "yes," but what wasn't he sure about? Was he thinking of Paige? Did he not want to get involved with someone else? "Sean, if you don't want this, I understand."

"That's not it," he said, his voice throaty, uneven. He stared at her lips, and slowly met her mouth again with his own, grazing her lips in a sensuous, unhurried way.

Those featherlight touches slowly gave way to something more urgent and intoxicating, and Darcy soon found herself unable to contain the passion she felt welling up inside her chest. Her fingers explored the front of his shirt to the exposed skin above the top button, and she swore it felt hot to the touch. She let her hand glide up and around to the back of his neck, and when she raked her fingers through the hair there, Sean's lips became more fevered.

Darcy had no idea how long the kiss lasted, maybe a minute or two, possibly five or more, because when he pulled away and drew a shaky breath, she felt as though she were coming up for air herself, from a deep, warm pool where she'd been for a pleasant eternity.

"I like this kind of retraining," she said, noting she'd slurred her words.

His eyes were heavy-lidded. "This is not part of the workday. We left that behind an hour ago."

"Really? So I'm not on the clock anymore?"

That half smile appeared again. "You're salaried, remember?"

"That's right." She licked her lips.

Sean nudged the packed cooler at the bottom of the blanket with his foot. "Hungry yet?"

A laugh rumbled at the back of her throat. "Not quite."

With that, Sean grinned and pulled her against him again, and Darcy found herself once again luxuriating in the depths of time forgotten.

Chapter Thirteen

☙❧

S ean turned up his coat collar as he walked out of an economic development council meeting in the community room of the J. Broman Library. The building was a state-of-the-art structure, running on solar power, and built of recycled steel, glass, and bricks from the old foundry. A local artist painted the foyer's full-wall mural of the flora and fauna of a Northwoods old-growth forest. It was stunning. He passed it on his way out the double doors, which led him onto Mill Street. Darcy would love it if she hadn't already seen it. He'd make a point of asking her tomorrow.

Since their time at the beach spot yesterday afternoon, he'd been thinking about Darcy nonstop. He couldn't count the number of times she'd caught his eye during the tour today. She even left a raspberry-filled long john from Debi's Donuts sitting on the dashboard of Clem first thing this morning. What was happening between them? It wasn't just a one-sided—what?—a crush on his part? Absolutely not. He remembered what it felt like with Paige when they first started dating. He'd never considered that a fleeting infatuation, and this...this felt like so much more. Whatever hesitation he'd had about getting involved so soon after what Paige put him through was almost nonexistent at the moment. And Darcy wasn't the type to throw herself at someone either. Somehow he knew that. She was too smart. It was certainly no crush.

The night had cooled considerably. To the west, a watercolor sunset tinted the sky with its customary late summer palette of gold, red, and indigo. Across the street, the glow of Two Tree Coffee beckoned him. Sean scanned faces of those he could make out inside the shop. He considered getting a cup to go, maybe a small or else he'd be up half the night. He trotted across the street and took in the electric coffeehouse vibe as he walked in, inhaling the rich scent of hot roasted beans.

Two women stood in line ahead of him, so he glanced around again, noting the people seated alone but working on laptops, the women gathered in groups of two and three engaged in lively conversations, and a couple, huddled over their steaming mugs, talking in low voices. The space was an eclectic mix of upholstered armchairs, repurposed pallets turned into tables, local art, and strings of white lights, creating a warm tapestry of whimsy and cool.

His attention was drawn to the far corner, up a few short steps, to a set of small, round tables sitting beneath a rowboat suspended from the ceiling by cables. Dim lighting, offset by candles flickering in golden orbs on the tables, made it hard to see, but there was no mistaking the mass of dark curly hair of the person seated at one of those tables. Sean leaned sideways to see around several patrons who were in his line of vision.

Yes, it was Darcy.

And Darcy was with Aidan Renaudin.

He turned away from them again. The two women in line debated their choice of a brownie or macadamia nut cookie, taking up more than their fair share of time. He sighed heavily and shoved his hands into his coat pockets. Sean chewed on the inside of his cheek and silently fumed. Should he go over and say hello? Or wave on his way out the back door? Why was this such an issue anyway? Certainly she could have a damned coffee with whomever she wanted.

Finally, the women moved out of his way.

"Can I help you?" The barista's fingers hovered over the keypad.

"Small coffee. That's it." He fished money from his wallet, let it fall to the counter.

Darcy's back was to Sean, so he watched them while he waited. Aidan gestured wildly as he talked to her. His facial expressions grew more animated. He leaned forward, touched her arm, threw his head back, and laughed. Anyone could see Aidan Renaudin liked her. And for that reason alone, Sean despised him.

When his coffee arrived, he grabbed it full-fisted, despite the overly hot cup burning his hand. He stood there a moment longer, lobbing the reasons to interfere in their conversation or ignore them back and forth in his mind like a tennis match. He was about to leave, his better half winning out, when Aidan pointed to him and waved. Too late. Darcy turned and saw him too.

Take it easy. Don't let that fool know you're irritated.

Darcy got up, weaving between the tables, a tentative smile on her lips. Yes, she knew how he felt. She'd witnessed the heated conversation between him and Aidan at the retirement party. He'd reassure her it didn't bother him. But it did.

"Hey," she said, her hand brushing his when she approached. Eyes wide and shining, her expression lit something inside of him, and despite the readiness to ignore them moments ago—out of spite, feigned indifference, or something else—he felt nothing more than a deep longing to be with her. Darcy had awakened what Paige had almost obliterated.

Still seated at the table, Aidan studied his phone. Sean pulled his attention away from him and focused on Darcy. "How are you?" He lifted his chin in Aidan's direction. "Business meeting?"

"Of course. He's bound and determined to develop part of that beach on the property. He even said..." She stopped and her expression turned apologetic. "Maybe I shouldn't be talking about this. Ingrid's wanting to sell the place and all I'm doing is talking about the reasons that she shouldn't."

"I see nothing wrong with not wanting to tear up an already beautiful stretch of beach. To hell with lifeguard stands and beach umbrellas."

She hesitated and looked toward Aidan. "I'm just trying to keep my personal feelings out of this."

"I don't think I could do that."

Again, her smile faltered. "This is really an awkward position for me."

Sean felt himself soften. "I know. Maybe he'll realize that Hendricks isn't the resort-type community that he's picturing. Or maybe someone will steal it away from him. I don't trust him."

Darcy reached for his hand again. "I know. Hey, maybe we can have Rollie and Brandy meet on the trail again?"

"Do you think they'd mind if we tagged along?"

"I don't think they have much say in the matter," she answered. She let go of his hand but not before tickling his palm with her index finger and giving him a smile that almost set him on fire. "And if they do, it's too bad."

DARCY RETURNED TO THE TABLE WITH AIDAN WHO was simultaneously typing something on his laptop and talking into the phone, the device propped between his ear and shoulder. As she sat down again, he ended the conversation and set the phone on the table.

"I thought you said you two weren't dating?" Aidan didn't meet her eyes, as he was still preoccupied with whatever was on his screen.

Darcy tucked her hair behind her ears and watched Sean talk with a young couple seated at one of the tables near the front door. Sean clapped the guy on the shoulder before he headed outside. One of the things she loved most about him was how comfortable he seemed in the company of everyone he met. She supposed it was because of the tours.

When she was with him it was as if no one else in the world existed, that was how focused he was. Or maybe that was just with her. She warmed at the thought.

"We're not," she answered, watching Sean until he was out of sight.

"Really?" He grinned, but his good-natured demeanor didn't mask the uncertainty. He thought she was lying. "That was a really friendly looking exchange." He leaned back against the chair, finally focused on her. "But I get it. Like I said before, I'm not going to ask for another date. I would like you to consider another proposition though."

Her attention snapped back to Aidan. "Oh?"

"Yes. Hear me out before you say no." He closed his laptop with a perfunctory click.

Darcy crossed her arms across her chest. "Okay. Shoot."

"I've been very direct about my intentions for Blueberry Point Lodge. It's new to me, the hospitality aspect, even though I already own commercial property."

"You've been pretty thorough in your research, though. I mean, you're asking all the right questions. Between Ingrid and me, I hope you feel you're getting the answers you need."

He lifted his chin and looked at her with half-lidded eyes. "Yes, you've both been very helpful. Thanks for that. And here's my proposal: when it's up and running, you come back to Blueberry Point Lodge to an expanded role," he said, his eyebrows raising as he put an emphasis on "expanded."

Darcy was intrigued. "What do you mean by that?"

He leaned forward, resting his elbows on the table. "I'd like you to manage it."

"That would be no different than the role I had before."

"I guess I haven't made myself clear about how Blueberry Point Lodge is going to change. Despite what your friend says about restrictions and preservation—"

"It's Sean."

"Yes, him. I think my plans for the place are going to bring a lot of revenue into town. That's never a bad thing."

Darcy wanted to say that it could be, especially if the one thing that brought visitors to Hendricks—its scenic, natural beauty—was forever altered. There had to be restrictions on the environmental impact in a place that had shoreline access. Had Aidan even checked into that?

"Anyway, I've talked to Ingrid about what you were making there. I'm prepared to double it."

"What?!" She nearly choked. Darcy also realized she'd shouted since several heads turned in their direction. "How can you even offer me that at this point?"

Taken aback at her surprise, Aidan glanced around at the other tables then laughed. "You think I'm playing with you?"

She hesitated. "Yeah, basically, I do."

"What if I were further along with the plans? Then would you consider it?"

Darcy huffed. "I'd be a fool to turn that down." She shrugged. "But then, I'm not above making foolish mistakes."

He gave her that overdone smoldering look again. "Hard to believe. You seem like the type that has had her whole life mapped out since birth."

"I'm focused but not that obsessive."

"It would save you from having to ride that fish bus," he said with a smirk.

At that, Darcy felt a twinge in her chest. "It's not that bad. Kind of gimmicky, but the guests love the buses."

Aidan hitched his shoulder dismissively. "Then you'll think about it?"

"Yes, I'll at least consider the offer, though I still think it's a little premature."

"Let me worry about the finances. Ingrid's ready to sell. The sooner the better, she told me the other day."

Darcy hated that it was moving so quickly, and now the pressure of a very lucrative job offer. Still, she wasn't *committing* to it, just considering his proposal.

But despite Aidan's phenomenal offer, Darcy couldn't imagine leaving Sturgeon Widows Tours for such a position. How could she ever quit and work for a competing business in a town this size? She'd be vilified. And then there was Sean. What was happening between them? Where would it go? They seemed so compatible, but she knew that any involvement with this project of Aidan's would spell disaster for them at this early stage. She wouldn't mention Aidan to him anymore. Sean obviously didn't like him, and with good reason. The more she spoke with Aidan, the more it seemed that Aidan wanted Sturgeon Widows Tours to go away too.

Chapter Fourteen

❧❦❧

One of the reasons Darcy moved to Hendricks—aside from the constant needling from Bethany—was the beckoning of its laid-back, outdoorsy vibe like she'd told Sean. The town owed the lake, streams, and forested trails for that culture, and the subsequent shops filling in the storefronts on Mill and Main Streets were indebted too. Outfitters, bait shops, boat dealers, and bike rental stores catered to those using the trails and rivers year round. Even when the fall visitors left the North Shore after the colors turned, the locals took advantage of the solitude outdoors. Off-season population numbers hovered around 2,000, yet the ruddy-cheeked, hardy people remaining weren't daunted by the frigid temperatures and frequent snowfall in the darkest hours of winter. Stream fishing and biking gave way to cross-country skiing and snowshoeing in Tettegouche State Park. Darcy loved that the landscape invited her to try activities she'd never had a chance to before while living in Chicago and Marquette.

She and Sean agreed to meet on "his" trail a few mornings later—the Sage River trail, near his cabin and a two-mile walk to Sheevy's Lake—after she'd asked him if he'd like to spend an afternoon hiking. He'd bring his fly rod and give her a lesson. They'd take the dogs. She'd supply the picnic lunch this time around, and maybe they'd actually eat what they packed this time, unlike Wednesday night on the beach. Her skin prickled at the memory.

At the trailhead, Darcy opened her car door and Rollie bounded over her lap and into the gravel parking lot. Sean was already there, lifting his rod case from the bed of his truck. Brandy weaved figure eights between him and the truck until she saw Rollie. Then the two dogs were nose to nose in an instant like long-lost friends.

Darcy watched the dogs, amused. "Such good buddies already."

"Brandy is pretty low-key. Not much riles her."

"That's a good trait for a dog."

Sean tossed the case onto his shoulder. "A good trait for anyone."

The dogs ran ahead of them on the path, though she didn't trust Rollie off leash. When the dog reached the end of his retractable leash and stopped short, he gave Darcy a withering look.

They walked along the path, which was cloaked in its autumnal carpet—reds, golds, and russet leaves crunching under their footsteps. The chill of winter wasn't far off as Darcy could feel its fingers prying against the bare skin above her coat collar. As they hiked in silence, she wondered if Sean felt as at ease with the lack of conversation as she did. She glanced at his profile and found his expression relaxed but inscrutable. Until he realized she was staring at him. He smiled and reached for her hand.

"What are you looking at?"

"You. Just wondering what's in your head."

Sean chuckled. "Nothing too heavy. Work, what I'm doing with the cabin." He looked up into the trees, and paused. "You."

"Me?"

"Of course."

He didn't elaborate though Darcy wished he would. The more time she spent with Sean, the more she found herself thinking about his quiet nature. Was his silence a good sign, charged with daydreams and desire? Or was it filled with regret and indecision.

They came to a small clearing along the Sage, where the foliage grew sparse and the soil along the river looked tamped down from others using it as a fishing spot. Sean clipped a tie-out cable on Brandy and looped it around a young birch. Darcy did the same with Rollie.

"Ready for a lesson?" he asked, handing her a box of flies. "Pick one."

When their hands brushed as they passed the box, though, the contact was electric. His eyes burned into her and she almost took a step back at their intensity, the look was that intoxicating. He withdrew the box slowly from her hand as if any sudden movement might break the spell, and slipped it back into the pocket of his coat.

Darcy glanced down at the disappearing box. "So fishing can wait?"

Sean's fingers intertwined with hers. "If that's okay with you," he said. His eyes held her prisoner, twin pools of green and gold, taking on the hues of the forest around them—mesmerizing, rich, and seductive.

She stepped into him, and his hands ran up her arms and enfolded her into his embrace. The tickling touch of his mouth grazed her bottom lip once, twice, before he hungrily covered hers with his own, causing her to inhale sharply, and an overwhelming need swelled within her as if it were squeezing the very breath from her body.

After several minutes, Brandy barked, which prompted Rollie to start yapping too. The dogs obviously didn't like her and Sean's attention elsewhere. Reluctantly, Darcy pulled away when the cacophony of barking grew obnoxious. She was still close enough to feel Sean's breath on her face, and those eyes, dark-lashed and penetrating, searched hers. He arched an eyebrow.

"That wasn't the lesson I had in mind, but I'm not complaining," he said, his voice husky.

Darcy smiled and stepped back. She touched her lips, savoring the feel of his kiss. The sensation was short-lived, though, as Rollie tugged on her pant leg. She took a treat from her jacket pocket and offered it to him. Rollie swallowed his whole. Brandy, showing impeccable canine manners, muzzled her hand and gently took the biscuit into her mouth.

She looked at Rollie. "Someone needs a behavior lesson."

Sean winced. "I hope you're not talking to me," he said lightheartedly.

"Not you. This dog."

"He probably needs a little socialization," he said. "Brandy might be good company for that." He knelt down to organize the fishing gear. Darcy followed his cue as she sat on the soft carpet of cedar flags a few feet away on a small rise to watch the river rush by. The water, clear and unforgiving, looked cold. Darcy shivered.

Sean unzipped the rod case and set the pieces beside him on the ground. Watching him, it occurred to Darcy that she didn't want a fishing lesson. If he offered again she'd feel obligated, but what she really wanted was something she hesitated to bring up, and that was the real story about what had happened between him and Paige. If the breakup was as bad as everyone hinted at, he probably wouldn't want to share it with her. But she also felt that she needed to know, if she and Sean were to move beyond the kissing-in-remote-places thing and start a real relationship.

Sean took off his jacket and settled the fleece over her shoulders, though not before he pulled the fly box out of his pocket and opened the lid. He sifted through the flies with his index finger. He looked over at her then, the skin between his eyebrows creasing.

"I'm not one to talk, but you seem extra quiet," he said.

She glanced sideways at him and hitched a shoulder.

His face grew more serious. "I didn't do anything...to upset you?"

"No, not at all."

An awkward silence settled between them. In the quiet,

the leaves above them rustled with impatience. Brushstrokes of clouds drifted beyond the treetops. Somewhere a gull cried. Then Sean said, "I love this river."

Darcy took a deep breath. "Me too. It's very peaceful."

He looked at her again as if he expected her to say something else so she took advantage of the moment.

"If only everything was as transparent as the water."

He feigned a grimace. "What does that mean?"

She smiled, hoping to ease some of the tension knotting her stomach. "We're both wondering what the other is thinking."

"What do you want to know about me?"

She flexed her hand, realizing she had it balled into a fist. "I hope this isn't prying. Tell me if it is, but I'm wondering what happened with you and Paige."

He looked at the water again. Did his brow dip at the mention of Paige? Or was it only a shadow that passed over his face?

"There's not much to tell. We dated for about a year. She had a serious accident but eventually recovered. We broke up after that." He snapped the lid of the fly box closed and stuffed it into the rod case. He yanked the zipper closed on that, too, a little too forcibly.

Though he spoke so matter-of-factly, Darcy could hear the hesitation in his voice, and the mental filtering taking place behind the disclosure. He was holding back. And he was irritated.

Darcy glanced at him. "Okay."

He opened his mouth then pressed his lips together again as if he wanted to add something but thought better of it. After a few moments, he sighed. "We loved each other at first. Well, for a short while." He shook his head dismissively. "But then it turned into something different, not love at all. Quite the opposite. At least that's how I felt." He looked at her and shrugged.

"What changed?"

"She wanted to go places far from here. Constantly."

"You don't like to travel?"

His brow furrowed when he looked at her. "It's not that I don't. It's just that this job doesn't allow me to get away much."

"I see."

He continued to watch her. "Do you see where that would cause problems?"

She nodded, though apparently not convincing enough, because he leaned forward so he could look her full in the face.

"I have to be here. We're a small company," he said.

"I get it. But for someone who likes to go places, I can see where that would be a point of contention."

Sean scratched at the back of his neck. "Point of contention," he said quietly. "Yes, I suppose it was that."

Darcy wanted more from him. When he looked away and shook his head, she knew that's all she'd be hearing on the subject. Maybe at some point he'd open up again. She drew her knees against her chest and struggled with finding the right words, a response that encouraged more discussion in the future. The last thing she wanted to do was end this small revelation on a sour note. A door had opened.

She rocked back, still encircling her knees with her arms.

"Love should be like this water—clear, fresh, sometimes tempestuous, never stagnant," she said in a hushed tone. "Dependable, full of life."

Sean whooped. "You clearly haven't seen it in March and April during the snowmelt. It can be murky, unpredictable. Downright dangerous," he said, picking up a rock next to his hip. "Like love." He tossed the rock across the water, hitting the far bank.

Darcy wanted to argue, to turn his pessimistic worldview of love on its head and *show* him what she meant. But more than anything, his words stung. There she gave him her heartfelt version of what she thought love was and he chose to make a joke.

"Speaking of love, I'll be at the Osgood wedding on Saturday," he said.

She pressed her lips together, resigned to having the topic of Paige closed for the time being. Maybe that door to understanding their relationship hadn't opened all that much. "I know. You're officially on the guest list this time."

Sean smiled. "Need any help between now and then?"

"There's really not much you can do. I have to be there on Thursday night when the wedding party comes to decorate."

"I can bring my decorating toolkit," he said, rubbing his hands together.

"You have a kit for decorating wedding receptions?"

"Sure do. In a small town like Hendricks, people call on each other all the time for help with that kind of stuff."

"Good to know."

"Besides, after you finish, I thought we could go to the

lighthouse. It's supposed to be a full moon Thursday. Sometimes when the moon hits the water just right, you can see the *Lianthia*," he said, sifting rocks through his fingers. "I know a path down to the beach there."

"You and your secret paths."

"I know all of them," he said and winked.

"Sounds like a plan."

Darcy swung her backpack from where it sat behind her to her lap. She unzipped the main compartment and unloaded Tupperware, bags of chips, and the homemade mint chocolate chip cookies she'd baked last night.

He watched her empty the contents of the pack. "You're ready for lunch so soon?"

She snapped off the container lids then dug in her pack for the plastic utensils. "I probably should get back sooner rather than later. Working two jobs is taking its toll on my apartment."

Sean searched her face when she met his eyes. "You're sure everything is all right?"

She might have hesitated a second or two too long before answering, and no, she wasn't sure everything was all right, but she smiled back at him.

"Perfect," she said, thinking about how deftly he'd pulled that door closed just as soon as she'd cracked it open.

Chapter Fifteen

Emily slid a pink-and-gold box onto the table in the lobby on Tuesday morning. Outside, a bitter October rain beat against the windows. Darcy pulled her cardigan tight around her to ward off the dampness she felt even though they were warm and dry inside.

"Fresh pot of coffee is on too," Emily said, opening the lid. The smell of Debi's Donuts hit Darcy's senses with a sweet wave of heaven. She grabbed one and licked the glaze off her fingers just as Sean came out of his office. The look in his eyes and the way his lips curved into a wicked grin told Darcy he had more on his mind than her frosted fingers.

"This is consolation for what I'm going to ask you to do today," Emily said, looking especially guilty. "The Davis family cancelled their tour this morning. I guess half the family is sick. They'll reschedule, the grandmother said. Sooo...that leaves us with three empty hours."

Darcy poured herself a cup of coffee with her free hand. "What do you need me to do?"

Sean's mother glanced sheepishly at the shoulder-high stack of cardboard boxes in the corner behind the counter. "Well, those came out of your office before it became an office. We're horribly behind getting the information about former guests into our new database. I'd like to pull emails and addresses for a mailing list. Then we'll recycle the paper copies." Emily shoved her sleeves up to her elbows before hoisting a box from the pile and setting it on the counter between her and Melina. She looked at Darcy. "Let me show you what I want, then I'll let you get to work."

Melina leaned back in her chair. "Thank goodness! I've been working on these files in my spare time for the last month. Not getting anywhere either," she said.

Sean heaved another box from the pile. "Don't ever think my mother is beneath bribery. The donuts are excellent currency."

Emily looked at her son. "What are you doing?"

"I'm helping, of course. I thought I could weed out from the files what Darcy needs to enter in." He shrugged.

"I thought you were working on the new brochure?" said Emily, her forehead furrowing. Darcy didn't miss the teasing lilt in her voice though. She knew by the dropped hints over the last three weeks that Emily would like nothing more than to see her spend extra time with Sean.

"I was. Finished it and emailed it to the printer just now."

Melina looked aghast. "How come you never read to me? That would make this go so much faster."

Darcy turned her back so Melina wouldn't see the smile she couldn't suppress. She waited for Sean to answer, wondering how he'd extract himself from that one.

"You type so fast I didn't think it'd make much difference," he said finally. He didn't wait for her response, but instead carried the box into Darcy's office and set it on the floor. To Darcy, he said, "I'll wait in here while you talk to Emily." His lips twisted into a smile before he sat in the spare chair in her office.

Darcy gave him the thumbs up as she settled next to Melina. Emily pulled up her own chair and opened the first file that she pulled from the box.

"All we need for our records is the name, physical address, and an email if they gave us one," Emily said, pointing to the spreadsheet Melina already had opened. She read the information to Melina, whose fingers flew over the keyboard as she inputted it. "Where is Gwinn, Michigan, anyway?"

Darcy looked at the folder in front of Emily. "It's southeast of Marquette about twenty miles."

Melina looked sideways at her. "Are you from Michigan?"

"I went to school there. At SEMMI."

"That's right. After the Coast Guard," Melina said.

Darcy hadn't told Melina about those details. She could only guess that Melina and Emily had talked about her qualifications before hiring her.

"We're very lucky to have someone like Darcy here," said

Emily. "With her experience on the water and that internship you told me about—amazing!"

Melina smiled thinly while focusing on the screen. "I'm surprised you found your way to a job like this."

Emily gaped at the younger woman. "What's that supposed to mean? This company isn't exactly menial labor."

Darcy straightened in the chair. "I love history and the water. This place is the perfect fit."

Melina finished typing and dropped her hands into her lap. "I didn't mean it like that. What I was trying to say was that usually people who go to SEMMI go on to graduate school to specialize." Melina got up to get a donut.

Behind Melina's back, Emily's eyes momentarily widened when she glanced at Darcy. She mouthed "sorry" as she pushed her glasses to the top of her head. A few seconds later, she touched Darcy lightly on the arm. "I don't mean to pry, but is graduate school still a possibility? We'd hate to lose you."

Darcy didn't answer right away. Emily was her employer, after all, and Darcy didn't want it to seem like she wasn't completely vested in working there. While Darcy had never ruled out the chance that she'd return to school, settling down into a job she loved, the *right* job, made the prospect dimmer as time went on. But she owed Emily an honest answer.

She shrugged. "Truthfully, I still think about it."

Emily feigned a frown. "I don't want to discourage dreams by any means, but we really like you here," she whispered.

Darcy heard the emphasis on "we" and thought of Sean. "Thank you. I'm happy to hear that."

"And I say 'we' because—"

It was Darcy's turn to whisper. "I know who you mean, Emily."

"I thought you might," she said, pointing her finger toward Darcy's office where Sean waited, out of sight.

Smiling, Darcy said in a normal tone. "I like it here. It feels like home, but I can't do both obviously. The program I'd been looking at is in North Carolina." She paused again and took a deep breath. "I'm not sure I'm up for moving again, starting over."

"That's a big decision."

"Still, it's tempting. And my family, well, my mother actually, adds to the pressure about going back."

"Mothers tend to do that, don't they?" Emily raised her hand. "Guilty."

Darcy smiled. "Silly me for thinking it would stop well before I hit my mid-twenties."

"Oh, honey. It'll never stop." Emily patted the top of her hand. "But I understand. It sounds like you still have some thinking to do."

Emily and Darcy turned in their seats when they heard a chair creak in Darcy's office. In the doorway, Sean stood there, wearing an unreadable expression.

"Going out for a while," he said as he walked through the lobby, ignoring the protests of his mother that they had work to do.

SO SHE WAS THINKING OF LEAVING TOWN?

Sean yanked open his truck door, simultaneously turning the key in the ignition and buckling his belt. He couldn't get away fast enough.

He'd heard only parts of the conversation between Darcy and his mother, but they were important parts, namely that Darcy still considered graduate school a possibility, and that it would take her far from Hendricks.

Idiot! He should have known better than to fall for her, especially after what happened with him and Paige. He swore he wouldn't bother with relationships for a long, long time, not after what Paige put him through. Why didn't he notice that Darcy and Paige were so similar—restless, commitment-shy women who had big plans, plans that didn't include staying in one place for very long? Of course Darcy had given him all of the right answers when he asked her what she loved about Hendricks that day at the beach. She was their company's tour guide. They'd hired her because she was fantastic at selling Hendricks to visitors. But what she didn't say was critical to any future they might have together, and that was that she planned to stay.

Sean drove east out of town and didn't really have a destination in mind until he ended up at Blueberry Point Lodge. The tires crunched on the serpentine gravel drive as he made his way to the carriage house. The Callahan's Explorer was gone. Good. That would save him the trouble of having to explain what he was doing there. That he had no idea what led him there would have made an interesting explanation, indeed.

But he did know what led him here. It started as a seed

of an idea weeks ago when Emily mentioned Ingrid's plans to close Blueberry Point Lodge to guests and eventually sell. When Renaudin arrived in town unexpectedly shortly afterward, all because Ingrid felt obligated to show him the property—family ties and all that—the idea took root. Sean had turned it around in his conscience since then, examining it from all angles, thinking about its feasibility.

Sean turned off the truck, opened the door, and breathed deeply, inhaling the scents of cedar, algae, and decaying leaves caught in the undergrowth of downed branches and pools of rainwater in the forested plot of land just beyond the yard. Over the slight ridge, the lake threw wave after wave against the shore in angry protest. Thinking all of what lay before him—the house, the wooded lot, the private cove—would be inaccessible if that fool Renaudin bought the place made his head hurt. If Renaudin thought he could breeze into Hendricks and steal property with such close ties to the Stetman family, and then turn it into something unrecognizable, well, it was unimaginable. Sean would have fun sending him on his way.

Aidan Renaudin buying Blueberry Point Lodge wasn't really fueling his anger at the moment though. He knew that. That issue would be resolved with a phone call, one he intended to make as soon as he met with Emily and Melina later in the week. No, it was a catalyst for what really bothered him, and that was the conversation he'd overheard between his mother and Darcy.

Shoving his hands in his coat pockets, Sean made his way along the path through the low-bush blueberries. Their leaves, a deep crimson, rustled in harmony with those of a single aspen overhead. He closed his eyes momentarily and wished for what he had wanted a month ago: to take a long break from the tour company.

What was he going to do? With each passing day since she'd joined Sturgeon Widows Tours, Darcy implanted herself within his heart little by little. The lilting sound of her voice as she talked with guests, her confident, adventurous spirit, and even her level of knowledge about the lake environment, captivated him. It was unfair to compare her to Paige really except, of course, that they didn't want to stay in one place.

Sean came to where the path descended to the beach, to the private cove he'd shown Darcy last week. Instead of following the path, he climbed one of the two boulders that flanked the trail, and finding the top of it relatively flat, sat down to think while the water churned and tossed itself twenty feet below.

Their weekend hike along the Sage hinted at trouble, though he hadn't noticed it at the time. She'd asked him about Paige, then cut their time together that afternoon short, saying she had work to do. He didn't want to talk about Paige, didn't see how she was relevant to him and Darcy. But then she'd mentioned that Paige's passion for travel and his inability to do so because of his job was an obvious "point of contention." He didn't mistake the indifference on her face when he said it wasn't possible for him to take time off like Paige had wanted. Was she testing him because she shared Paige's view?

Sean almost talked himself out of getting involved with her weeks ago, even brushing off his brother's jokes about he and Darcy dating. Of course he'd known better. Why didn't he listen to his gut? And what now? Were they destined to work together until she gave her notice who knew when? If there was one thing that was certain, Sean couldn't work side by side with Darcy and forget about what they'd shared. To pretend she was only a coworker after he'd opened up to her like he did would be his undoing. Maybe buying the property would be an opportunity to stay away from her. He'd insist his mother hire another driver—they'd be expanding their employee base anyway with the addition of the house—and it would free him to make some of the needed repairs that Henry hadn't been able to tackle since his health declined.

Yes, that was it. Sean simply would stay out of the picture until Darcy did inevitably leave. And in hindsight, he didn't doubt that she would.

Sean drove back to the office after dinner since he'd left his phone charging in his office. Certain the place would be empty, he was surprised to see the lobby light on when he parked in front.

Melina.

"What brings you back here?" she asked when he walked in.

"Forgot something."

He unplugged the phone, stuck it in his pocket, and stopped at the desk, wondering what kept Melina working so late.

"Just catching up on a few things," she said vaguely. She shuffled some papers while she studied him. "Is everything all right?"

"Sure. Why?"

"Oh, I don't know. You left so quickly this afternoon. We wondered what happened."

Sean avoided looking at her. He wasn't sure he could hide the lie. "I had an appointment that I almost forgot about."

Melina brightened. "Oh, that's good. I was afraid you were upset about...something." Her eyes lingered on his when he finally glanced at her. She tilted her head.

"Nope. I'm good." He turned to leave.

"Sean?"

"Yes?" He faced her again.

"I'm going to grab a sandwich. Want to join me?"

"Thanks, though I think I'm just going to head home."

Disappointment clouded her face. She opened her mouth to say something but dropped her gaze instead. Melina set the papers on the counter. When she looked up again, she smiled though it was a forced one. "So how do you think Darcy is working out?"

Puzzled, he looked at her. "Fine. Why?"

Melina shifted her weight. "She hinted to Emily and me today that she might not be sticking around for much longer."

Sean feigned surprise. Melina didn't need to know that he'd overheard the conversation. "Where is she going?"

"She's considering graduate school on the East Coast somewhere."

"So, it's nothing definite."

Melina frowned. "Well, no. But I thought you might need to know something like that."

"Thanks for the heads-up."

Again, she studied him. The corners of her mouth dipped slightly. "Maybe we can get a sandwich or coffee sometime soon?"

"Maybe soon. See you tomorrow," he said before walking out the door into the clear, cold night.

Chapter Sixteen

fter a brisk walk around town with Rollie the following Saturday afternoon, Darcy shuffled through papers stacked haphazardly across her dining room table trying to find one page of notes in particular. She sifted through the mound several times, creating a bigger disaster, but the one page was still missing —her event timeline for that night's reception. If it were as easy as printing a new one, she would have done it already and been out the door. But the missing page was covered with handwritten notes, crucial add-ons like the revised times for the deejay, cake-cutting, the names of the wedding party, and a last-minute list of song requests from the bride herself. She had to find that list.

Outside, the cloudless, crisp day competed with the brilliance of the lake. The gloriousness of it made the heaviness Darcy felt in her chest even more unfair, though it was her own fault. Had she kept her professional and private life separate, she'd be thinking only of the night ahead and not how Sean hadn't spoken to her since he rushed out of the office on Tuesday afternoon. He drove the bus each of the last three days but stayed ominously silent during the tour and in the office. Even Melina noticed.

"What happened between you two lovebirds?" Melina had asked as she and Darcy left the office yesterday afternoon.

Darcy sensed the self-satisfied air before Melina even said anything. She'd worn that pursed-lipped smile around the office all week. "I really don't want to talk about it, Melina."

"He wasn't anywhere near ready to start dating again. I called that weeks ago, didn't I?"

Darcy replayed Melina's words in her mind over and over again. Melina warned her about Sean. She hated Melina was right.

The list wasn't in the backseat of her car either. She pushed around boxes of party favors, hand-painted beach cobbles done by a local artist friend of the groom's mother, hoping to find the paper tucked underneath. No luck. Nor was the list hiding under any of the empty plastic bags, the backpack, or the pile of clean rags she needed to return to Blueberry Point Lodge. There was one last place to check— her office.

When she pulled alongside the building a few minutes later, she was surprised to see Sean's truck parked in its usual spot. Dread knotted her stomach. She didn't want to see him just yet. The wedding and reception were hours off, and she'd be forced to spend enough time with him there.

Maybe she could rush in, check her desk, and leave quickly without him even realizing she'd come in.

She eased the side door open and slipped in. She froze.

Sean and Melina sat side by side at the round table in the lobby. They looked up when the breeze from the open door rearranged the papers spread before them.

Darcy felt her face flush. "I—I came for something." Stupid. She didn't need to explain herself. It was her workplace too.

Melina smiled conspiratorially. "You're not interrupting anything," she said, though Darcy could tell she didn't mind being caught alone in the office with Sean by her smug expression. In contrast, Sean's focus returned to the business before him.

In her office, the missing page lay atop her file cabinet. Darcy grabbed it and hurried back into the lobby, eager to be away from the place. She glanced again at Sean. He couldn't even meet her eyes. It was as if she weren't even there.

It struck Darcy in that instant that whatever she thought was starting between Sean and her had been overblown in her own mind, and maybe a regrettable mistake in his. His expression as he looked at her when she walked into the lobby had been devoid of the warm intensity and humor that she'd found so attractive in the last month. What had happened to that person? Well, what did it matter? Hadn't she decided to keep their relationship professional anyway, before her lapse in judgment? Now she had her wish.

Darcy spent the next several hours immersed in last-minute conversations with the vendors and bridal party, and thankfully with not a minute to spare for ruminating on the situation. Though she wasn't technically a wedding planner, she'd overseen enough events at Blueberry Point Lodge to know how to ease jitters. So when the bride, Justine Osgood, popped her head out of the room where she and her five bridesmaids gathered, and motioned frantically for her, Darcy calmly walked over.

Justine, a petite former college swimmer who'd grown up in nearby Dentsen, was near tears. "I cannot believe this just happened." She held up a satin pump, minus its heel. "It just popped off. What am I going to do?"

"What size are you?"

"Seven," said Justine, tossing the shoe and its heel onto a heap of clothes and makeup bags strewn over a love seat in the corner of the room.

"I think we're in luck."

Darcy called Ingrid, who was somewhere in the house. When she explained the situation to Ingrid, the older woman came downstairs within the minute, a pair of tiny-heeled, rhinestone-studded sandals in hand. Justine saw them and clasped her hands together.

"Total lifesavers, you two," she said before closing the door on the room again.

Darcy shook her head. "I thought you two were the same size. I guess it pays to go shoe shopping with your boss."

Ingrid chuckled. "I sure will miss working with you on these things, near catastrophes and all." Ingrid hooked her arm through Darcy's and the two women walked toward the foyer.

"Me too. Somehow I doubt Aidan could have come to the rescue in this situation. I can't imagine his management style will be as relaxed as yours and Henry's."

Ingrid stopped and faced Darcy, a puzzled frown turning the corners of her mouth down. "Aidan? Why would he...?" Then her expression changed to one of understanding. "I see. Didn't Emily—?"

Darcy's phone buzzed and she looked at the message on her screen. "We'll talk later. Looks like I'm needed outside in the tent."

"I'll see you in a few minutes," Ingrid said before busying herself with her own phone. "Call if you need me again."

The large white tent erected on the lawn shone like a pearl against the backdrop of the lake. As much as she loved the house, Aidan was right. Its boxy rooms didn't accommodate large events like weddings. She hoped when he did decide to build a structure for the larger events on the property that it didn't interfere with the view from the house. Her favorite spot was in the upstairs parlor in front of the arched window. There she liked to sink into the overstuffed armchair and prop her feet up on the window ledge with a cup of coffee. Her favorite spot for morning breaks, the chair afforded a priceless view of the lake.

As she spoke with the members of the ensemble near the front of the tent, guests milled around the white folding chairs, choosing seats. Darcy looked down at herself momentarily, having forgotten if she had already changed into her dress. She smiled to herself and smoothed the sequined fabric over her stomach. Thank goodness.

When she looked up, Sean stood an arm's-length away.

How long had he been standing there, watching her? Her mouth went dry. She steadied herself against the back of a chair.

His hands were in his trouser pockets. "You look beautiful," he said flatly. He said it so quietly his words didn't register at first.

"Thank you."

If he hadn't been ignoring her for the past three days, Darcy certainly would have loved the compliment. His words combined with the physical presence of the man before her, the classy ruggedness accentuated by the plum shirt and plaid bow tie, making him look awkward and desirable all in the same glance, confounded her. He didn't look at all uncomfortable or sorry for slighting her. His demeanor was that of someone who had simply moved on.

He shifted his weight from one foot to another. "How do you do it?

She looked around. "What?"

"Everything is so...organized."

"That's my job."

His eyebrows dipped and he looked up at the house. "You're good at it."

Irritated, she wanted to leave, focus on the ceremony, which was only minutes away. "I have to get back to work."

He swept his arm to the side. "I'm not stopping you."

Darcy turned her back on him so he couldn't see the range of emotions, which surely played across her features. She checked the time on her phone, willing the hours to fly by as she walked away, a heaviness sitting at the back of her throat.

SEAN COULD BARELY STAND MOST OF THE MUSIC
selections the deejay played with irritating frequency. It was
all pop garbage—fast, fist-bumping, bass-thumping techno
music. He wasn't sure what he would have chosen instead,
but that wasn't it.

The tent glimmered with strands of suspended white
lights. Crystal-laden birch branches sprouted from the
immense glass vases in the center of each table. Amid the
fairy-tale setting, Sean grew increasingly annoyed. It didn't
help that Darcy looked like she should be hosting one of
those televised awards shows rather than overseeing a
wedding reception. He simply couldn't take his eyes off her,
which was a large part of his aggravation. Since he'd talked
to her before the ceremony, she had yet to look at him once.
He didn't blame her. Before tonight, he hadn't spoken a
word to her that wasn't related to a tour.

His brother collapsed in the chair next to him, red-faced
and sweaty.

"You're as lively as ever," Matt teased, sliding a bowl of
mixed nuts in front of him. Several spilled over the side
onto the tablecloth.

Sean drummed his fingers on the table and looked away
from Matt toward the dance floor. Charles Osgood hugged
Justine and kissed her cheek as they finished their father-
daughter dance.

"How do you manage to find the most irritating thing to
say to me when I least want to hear it?" Sean threw half a

cashew at him. It bounced off his cheek and onto the table. Matt popped it into his mouth.

"That's why you love me." Matt took a handful of nuts, shaking them in his palm before he tossed them in his mouth. "Speaking of which, Mom said you and the lovely Miss Conti are on the outs. What'd you do this time?"

Sean tensed. "Mom has no idea what she's talking about. We were never together enough to be 'on the outs' as Mom says."

Matt huffed. "Please, dude. Who do you think you're talking to? I'm your brother, remember? The one who always saw that guilty hitch on your lips when you tried lying to me."

"My brother with a megaphone for a mouth."

Matt cupped his hands around his mouth like he was going to announce something to the room. Instead he mouthed "lighten up" in Sean's direction. Then he pointed a finger at him. "So you're saying you won't tell me anything because you're afraid I'll say something. Which means there IS something to tell."

Sean rested an elbow on the table and rubbed his forehead. He was getting a headache. "She's a lot like Paige."

"How so?"

"This isn't permanent for her. She has bigger ambitions."

"Seriously? That's too bad. Sorry, man."

Sean shrugged. "Like I said, we didn't get very far before we decided it wasn't a good idea."

The bridal party finished their obligatory dances and invited other guests onto the dance floor. Sean groaned inwardly. He hated dancing, remembering awkward hands and fleeting glances in junior high, which made him blush and trip over his words. Matt twisted in his seat, looking around the tent.

"Well, I'll tell you what. I'm going to ask her to dance now that you're not interested anymore. I'll be hated by every guy under seventy in here in about two minutes." He stood up and brushed his hands together. "Watch me."

Sean laughed despite his mood. If he wasn't positive that Matt was the complete opposite of Darcy's type, he'd be jealous. Still, when Matt strode across the floor and was hand in hand with Darcy within his self-prescribed time frame, Sean's throat constricted. He envied Matt, now the object of Darcy's attention. His mind filled with hazy images of their time together, images already beginning to fade like summer's breath.

He stood and pushed in his chair. They'd never miss him now that the deejay kicked the music up a notch. Blue and pink lights pulsed from the light show near the speakers as the overhead lanterns dimmed. Matt and Darcy disappeared farther into the crowd. Seduced by the upbeat mood of the guests around them, they kept dancing after the last slow number ended. He couldn't stand it one minute more and walked out of the tent and into the clear, cold night, under a sky littered with stars and one watchful moon.

Chapter Seventeen

꧁✿꧂

After a few hours of fitful sleep last night and even less the night before, Sean desperately needed more coffee to make it through the morning. He was so tired that he swore there were four-ounce sinkers resting on each eyelid. If it weren't for his mom's call at seven that morning, telling him she was staying home to fight a bug, he'd still be in bed. Sean reminded her of his appointment at the bank but reassured her he'd get there as soon as he could. Two tours were on the books that day. His exhaustion was palpable.

Sean pulled along the curb in front of Debi's Donuts and killed the engine. His hands slid over the steering wheel, gripping the smooth surface.

The morning was silent and gray. It was impossible to make out where the horizon ended and the water began as the fog melded the two together in a hazy shroud over the lake. Dampness curled around him, the kind of cold that seeps through clothes and into bones. For all he knew, the chill he felt had more to do with Darcy's feelings about him than the effects of the weather.

Inside Debi's, Georgia Mark and her toddler son had just picked up their donuts at the counter and made their way over to a corner table. Sean approached the counter, laying his keys on the laminate top in a noisy mound. Debi's smile looked pinched as she waited for his order.

"Good morning, Sean," she said, sounding a bit resigned.

"Cinnamon roll. To go."

Debi opened her mouth to say something, but then shook her head and turned her back to get his order.

Sean heaved a sigh. He kept telling himself he was finished thinking about Darcy, but then her face or something she'd said or done floated through his mind again. This time it was the long johns sitting innocently behind the plexiglass case, a reminder of the donut she'd placed on his dashboard two weeks ago.

Sean handed over a couple bills when Debi slid the bag across the counter. When Debi didn't take the money right away, he looked up.

"Saw you at the wedding Saturday night."

Sean smiled halfheartedly. "Good for Justine and the Osgoods, huh?

"Yes, her new hubby seems like a great guy." She continued to look at Sean. Then she threw her hands up. "Far be it from me to offer advice—"

"Then don't."

"—but there's nothing worse for business than personal turmoil. Believe me, I know," Debi said.

He almost protested but recalled her very ugly divorce from Tom, a guy he remembered from Sherman High School's offensive line when he played football. The guy had been massive but soft, easy to mow down even before the snap touched the quarterback's hands. After he and Debi split two years ago, the shop's hours became sporadic during the course of summer and fall. People speculated about whether she'd close. And then even though normal hours resumed and Debi kept the donut case fully stocked, her heart didn't seem in it. The glazed rings tasted bland, filled with regret instead of sugar and yeast, and the eclairs, her signature pastry, temporarily lost their sweet magic. So Sean couldn't deny business life and personal setbacks affected one other, not when he'd sampled it firsthand.

Debi poured a to-go cup of coffee and pushed it toward him on the counter even though he hadn't asked for one. "For ruminating." She winked at him.

"What's that supposed to mean?"

"Well, now that you asked," she started, pulling up a stool behind the counter and sitting purposefully, all ready to dispense her wisdom.

Sean grinned in spite of himself. "You just can't help yourself, can you?"

Debi patted his hand. "Honey, we've known each other since kindergarten. I couldn't keep my mouth shut then. What makes you think I can now?"

He glanced at Georgia and her son still at the corner table in their own world. Georgia snuck looks at her phone in between trying to keep the boy in his high chair, donut pieces off the floor, and chocolate glaze from covering everything within his reach.

Debi touched the top of his hand. "I couldn't help but notice it was just you and one other person at the wedding Saturday night."

"I'm not following."

"You and Darcy."

If he heard from one more person about how they thought he and Darcy belonged together, he'd move out of Hendricks himself. Some days it was downright obnoxious living in a small town.

"Don't say it was my mother who told you that we are —we were—"

Debi threw back her head and laughed, a throaty guffaw. "This time, no." She studied her nails for a few seconds, a dramatic pause. "No, Emily hasn't said a word, though that sounds just like her. And I told you, it was like watching the Hallmark Channel Saturday night. The looks between you two."

Now he knew that Debi was full of it. Darcy's attention had been everywhere but on him when he looked at her which had been every other minute.

"She won't be in town for long from what she's told me." He didn't like lying to Debi.

"Then she must be talking out of both sides of her face. She told me she's moving into Blueberry Point Lodge as soon as that Aidan guy buys it. He's going to let her run it."

"She told you that?"

"As sure as sugar in donuts, sweetheart."

"When exactly did she tell you that?"

Debi tapped her chin with a blue fingernail. "Earlier last week. She always comes in on Tuesdays and Thursdays."

A week ago. So she didn't intend to stick around Sturgeon Widows Tours for very long. But she didn't plan to leave Hendricks either. Why would Darcy want to work with Renaudin instead of him? And why on earth would Renaudin think the sale of Blueberry Point Lodge was a sure bet? The fool obviously hadn't considered the Stetman family getting in the way.

"She loves that place if it's any consolation."

"Really?"

"Yep. Told me she'd love to live there. That's probably the only way she can stand working for him. Said she would have bought the place herself if she could afford it."

He picked up his keys, jangling them impatiently. "How do you know so much about Darcy?"

Debi looked incredulously at him. "Never underestimate the disseminating power of a donut and coffee."

"Thanks, Debi. I owe you," he called over his shoulder as he headed toward the door.

Outside, he fished out his phone and dialed Matt's number.

Chapter Eighteen

꧁❧꧂

D arcy tossed off the covers and scowled at the time on her phone on Monday morning. Rollie, curled up on the comforter at her feet, sensed her irritation and rumbled his displeasure too. She glanced toward her windows opposite her bed where the soft light filtered through the cracks in the blinds. Another gorgeous day, another painful contradiction for how she felt inside.

"I don't want to go to work. Can I call in sick too?"

At the sound of her voice, Rollie wagged and got up only to collapse in a furry heap at her side. He nudged his head underneath her armpit. She couldn't help but smile at her dog's ability to make light of the situation.

"How about you go to work for me, and I'll stay here and sleep?"

He looked up at her, cocking his head to the side.

"I don't blame you. It's not the happiest place to be at the moment."

Though Darcy didn't expect a call from him yesterday, and calling *him* was completely out of the question, she checked her phone constantly. Every text, beep, and notification set her on edge, making her hopeful that it would be him, but knowing in her heart that he was finished with her. Forget the halfhearted compliment he gave her at the wedding or the fleeting glances across the room all night. He clearly hadn't been ready for a relationship, and she practically threw herself at him. Hopefully, Aidan would take over Blueberry Point Lodge in no time. Then she could cut her losses and move on.

An hour later, she parked in her usual spot on Rimrock Drive. Her pulse hammered at the thought of seeing Sean, but his truck was noticeably absent. A confusing mix of emotions flooded her mind. She didn't want to see him, but now that he wasn't there, she wondered where he could be.

Inside the lobby, Melina looked up and rolled her eyes when Darcy came through the door.

"Thank goodness someone else besides him showed up. I was beginning to think I'd have to run this place by myself today." She thumbed over her shoulder to the vicinity of the potted ficus tree in the corner.

It was Matt, looking every bit like a younger, clean-shaven, less-sullen version of his brother.

"Hey, Darcy! Long time no see. Looks like it's you and me today."

"Hi, Matt." She managed a smile even though his too familiar tone was irritating. She'd only talked to him once before she saw him at the wedding, and then he'd asked her to dance. Today of all days she didn't need to be subjected to his over-the-top circus clown cheerfulness. She wanted to be left alone, and almost laughed aloud at her predicament. There she was, ready to lead tourists around for three hours, and she wanted nothing to do with people.

Melina tapped a pen on the counter. "I need to clue you in on this tour," she said impatiently. She gestured to the file on the counter. "Can you come here?"

Darcy bit her tongue to keep from saying something she'd regret. Instead, she approached the counter and rested her elbows on the surface.

Melina gave her a leveled gaze. "You really did a number on him, didn't you?"

Darcy had had it with Melina's snide comments. "What do you mean?"

Melina looked at the ceiling and shook her head. "I mean that Sean has never left a message on the company answering machine saying he wouldn't make it into work for the day. Even when Paige was giving him grief, he showed up."

The last thing Darcy wanted was her involvement with Sean to affect business. That was never her intention. That's why she shouldn't have broken her policy of not dating people she worked with. She'd seen the effects of what could happen after her years in the Coast Guard. And the person that lost was usually the one with the most at stake.

Darcy straightened. "Whatever is keeping Sean away has nothing to do with me."

"'Whatever' indeed." Melina breathed a long and

exasperated sigh. "It doesn't matter. Here's what you're doing today."

While Melina proceeded to read the tour details for the morning, Darcy only half-listened. She'd read the pre-trip sheet later. Her mind was elsewhere, particularly how she could be proactive about the situation.

Maybe she'd start by apologizing to Sean for going after him when she'd known from the beginning that he didn't want to get involved. Yes, she'd clear the air and keep it professional until she could be back at Blueberry Point Lodge. Aidan's plan to make her the on-site manager solved the problem of signing another lease too. Then she'd go out of her way to avoid Sean Stetman as much as possible, though in a town the size of Hendricks she was bound to run into him somewhere—the trails, the donut shop, the coffeehouse, all of their favorite places. If only they weren't so compatible.

During her lunch break, she'd call Aidan too. They hadn't spoken since she met him at Two Tree Coffee more than a week ago. Maybe he could hasten the sale. Then she could give her notice to Emily sooner rather than later.

"Are you even listening to me?"

Melina's irritation was evident on her face when Darcy looked up.

"I'm not talking because I like the sound of my own voice, you know," Melina snapped. Then she took a deep breath. "You'll thank me for giving you a heads-up on this: one of the new male alpacas at the Loom & Lyre farm is loose inside the outer pen. They're trying to get him under control before we get out there. Fred Behar said if he and his two boys are still near the fence when you pull into the drive, that you're to take the group straight into the farm studio. He'll meet you there."

"Right." Darcy took the folder from Melina before pouring herself a coffee from the pot against the wall. She needed a pick-me-up desperately.

"Darcy?" Matt said over her shoulder. "We should get to the bus. It's time."

"Sure thing."

She didn't miss the glance between Matt and Melina when she turned around, though she didn't care that they thought her incompetent this morning. At the moment, throwing away this job for another, her third job in two months, was a real possibility. Her mother's concerns about her lack of responsibility would be justified, but Darcy would argue that it might save her own sanity. Sometimes responsibility had to take a backseat.

Outside, a brisk wind whipped around her and Matt, drawing the leaves into a mini-cyclone that skittered across the patio then deposited them against the brick wall. Darcy looped a thin scarf around her neck, and when the wind pushed back so that she had to try several times to adjust the fabric, she finally yanked it off and stuffed it into her coat pocket.

Matt noticed her agitation. "Are you all right?"

"No." She felt a twinge of sadness when she glanced at him. He looked so much like Sean. "I thought you were working at a job site?"

He hesitated. "Gas line ruptured. Forced to take the day off."

"And you decided to cover for your brother. How nice."

Matt stopped in front of the bus. "Whoa. I'm sensing serious hostility here. Don't tell me Sean is being his usual charming self."

Darcy pressed her lips together.

"Anything I can do?" Matt offered.

"Just help me get through this day."

He extended his arm toward the bus door, letting her get on first. She quickly gave the guests the tour safety talk, then settled into the seat behind Matt. They drove in silence until they passed the lighthouse. Loom & Lyre Alpaca Farm was another five minutes ahead.

Matt cleared his throat and spoke over his shoulder. "I'm going out on a limb here because, well, my brother's an idiot, but I love him nonetheless."

Darcy glanced at the back of his head and caught his look in the overhead mirror.

"I'm not asking you to be the rebound person. But be patient. It may seem like he doesn't care, but I know otherwise."

"What's that supposed to mean?"

"He's afraid you'll leave. Just like...the other one."

"You mean Paige? Why is everyone so afraid to say her name? It's like she's a communicable disease or something."

The corners of his eyes crinkled in the mirror. "Disease may be right, but definitely not contagious." Matt put on the signal to turn into the farm drive. "Personally, I couldn't stand her. Way too bossy."

"So you're saying he hasn't spoken to me in a week

because he's afraid I'm moving out of Hendricks? That's a strange way of getting me to stay."

"If you haven't noticed, my brother isn't the best at communicating. He'd much rather sulk and fish than face relationship problems."

"Maybe it's best that we didn't work out then. It doesn't sound like we operate the same way."

Matt pulled into a space along the front pasture. Sure enough, Fred and his boys were still trying to harness a brown alpaca who was not having any of it. Wild-eyed, the animal ran laps around the men.

"Berserk Male Syndrome," Matt said.

Darcy stood up to lead everyone from the bus. "Excuse me?"

"That's what's wrong with that guy."

"Berserk Male Syndrome? Is that a thing?"

"Sure is. It happens in llamas and alpacas sometimes when they've been overhandled by people."

Darcy huffed. "Maybe that's what's wrong with your brother."

Matt leaned back in his seat, chuckling. "Maybe I won't mention you said that."

She softened. Matt shouldn't bear the brunt of her frustration. "I'm sorry. I'm just very...hurt."

"I get it. I would be too."

The farm was one of her favorite stops. The animals, and the sunny studio and wool shop where Fred's wife, Joan, sold her products, were usually cleansing for Darcy. The woman's effervescent personality as she demonstrated spinning wool for the guests failed to lift Darcy's spirits, though. She wished Sean drove today. That way she could have apologized at some point, maybe during lunch, and put closure on the situation. Only then could she move on, and hopefully be relieved from the heaviness threatening to suffocate her since last week.

Chapter Nineteen

S ean timed his arrival to work that afternoon so he could get there right as the afternoon guests were ready to board Clem. He waited until the guests on the patio turned their attention to the front door, a signal that Darcy was walking outside to meet them. He hurried into the side lobby door so she wouldn't see him and met Matt inside.

He took Clem's keys from Matt. "Thanks. I owe you one."

Matt blew the air out of his cheeks. "Tell you what, I don't envy you one bit. She is not a happy camper, dude."

"I know that, but thanks for the reminder."

"If I were you I'd lay low for a while longer. She might not want to see your face just yet. She's hurting."

Sean glanced out towards the patio. He didn't like hearing that he was the reason for her pain. Yet he'd overheard her conversation with Emily. That had started it all. Defusing their misunderstanding needed to happen, well, yesterday. The sooner they talked, the better.

He clutched the keys in his fist, the cold metal biting into his palm. "I can't do that."

Matt shrugged. "It's your funeral."

When Sean climbed aboard the bus a few minutes later, Darcy's expression told him all he needed to know. He'd interrupted her mid-speech, her voice fading out as she watched him with her mouth hanging slightly opened while he landed in the driver's seat. After Clem roared to life, Sean eased the bus from the curb. He almost couldn't resist the temptation to check her reflection in the overhead mirror, but he waited until they were on Highway 61, heading east. It was then that he dared look at her. Sure enough, even from a distance, the steely set to her jaw was unmistakable. She was definitely angry. Matt had warned him.

The afternoon group, a senior citizen church group from Minneapolis requested the full seven-stop tour. The tour called for a one-and-a-half-hour trip west for three stops—the lighthouse and *Lianthia* site first, then to Red's for refreshments—before heading back east to catch the other stops. It took Darcy a few minutes to realize something wasn't right but when she did, Sean watched her move to the seat right behind him.

"When did you plan to inform me that the itinerary changed?" she hissed in his ear as they sped past the historic Flint Hills Motel.

"You don't seem like you're up for discussing things

lately." He didn't intend to slow down for the Sage River stop either, which was coming up fast on the left.

She huffed as they crossed the bridge. "So I'm supposed to wait and see where we stop before I launch into the tour script?"

"You're talented. It shouldn't be a problem," he said over his shoulder.

"You are just unbelievable. I sensed you had trouble communicating like a normal human being, but this just takes it to the next level," she said before she turned to face the guests. He listened while she filled them in on the company's history and hoped her hostility waned before he stopped the bus. If straying from the script upset her that much, she might be really annoyed at what he was about to do.

He put on his signal as they neared the driveway of Blueberry Point Lodge. Sean couldn't help a quick glance at Darcy. Sure enough, she was turning a darker shade of pink as she realized this stop wasn't even on the tour. He smiled to himself despite the fact that he might be wading into dangerous water.

While he normally waited until each guest exited the bus before he moved from his seat, especially since he'd taken over as driver, he didn't this time. Despite his gut somersaulting over itself, Sean stood and faced his guests.

"As you might have noticed while we were at the Sturgeon Widows Tours building a few minutes ago, there's no historical value there—no shipwreck, lighthouse, or famous salmon stream in sight. It's always just been a starting point for the tours. Our building is boring new construction, built from nondescript logs twenty years ago. It's a family business. My parents opened it in the nineties, and now my brother and I are official part owners." Sean paused. "That might spell trouble to anyone who knew us in high school, but we haven't burned the place down yet," he added with a smile.

The guests laughed while Darcy's face clouded with confusion. He kind of relished that—catching her by surprise—but he couldn't look at her for too long or he'd screw up.

He continued. "But it's a starting point for a different kind of venture, and that one started a month ago."

He stopped when Darcy stood up and came toward him, her anger once again unmasked. She shook her head, trying to get him to stop but not wanting to call attention to it. He could barely keep a straight face.

"That's not the script," she whispered.

"I can't remember the last time I looked at a script."

"Exactly! What are you doing?"

"I'm conducting the tour," he said calmly. "Or trying to anyway."

"This is not a stop."

"Can you just do your job and I'll do mine?"

"Narrating IS my job. You're just a driver," she said under her breath.

Face to face with her, Sean almost lost the battle to keep his plan intact. It was infuriating her, this straying off script. Improvising tour talks was what he excelled at, but it was a whole different ball game for someone like her who prized order and predictability. Darcy's eyes blazed into his.

He leaned in close, brushing her hair with his lips, breathing in that honeysuckle-and-cinnamon scent he'd come to long for, and whispered, "Sit down, Conti, and enjoy the tour."

Darcy drew back and stared at him. "Are you trying to make me quit?"

"On the contrary."

She studied his face for a few moments longer, then with her lips pressed together, stalked back to her seat. Was she too upset to respond to his next move? He breathed deeply. *I'll find out shortly.*

"So this spot that we're at today has a connection to my family. My great-grandparents used to live here. Then it was sold and it's been this perfect inn and venue spot for some of the larger events we have in Hendricks for more than twenty years."

The guests murmured approval as some of them peered out the windows toward the house. Darcy, arms crossed, sat silently in a seat two rows away. Exasperated, she slowly shook her head, refusing to look at him anymore.

"Sadly, the current owners are retiring from the hospitality business and selling. Fortunately for Hendricks, there is another business in town which prides itself on hospitality." He bowed slightly. "That would be Sturgeon Widows Tours."

"Now you might be thinking, 'What is he getting at?' and 'When are we going to get back to the tour?' Am I right? At least that's what my tour host, Miss Conti, is thinking."

Darcy looked up to the ceiling. She seemed resigned to

the fact that he wanted to make a fool of himself.

"Today is when my family and Blueberry Point Lodge converge once again. Your group is the first to know that we'll be signing the paperwork soon to repurchase the property. We're very happy that, in addition to the tours, our company finally has a place to house overnight guests, a service we've wanted to provide for quite a while. I'm excited, my family is excited, and I hope"—he finally looked at Darcy—"our tour host is excited, because she's a large part of the future here."

Darcy's expression changed from frustration to incredulity in an instant. Her mouth moved, trying to form words, but she only managed to sputter something unintelligible before her hand fluttered up to her mouth. She looked around, seemingly embarrassed or too stunned to do anything but sit there. Now that he had her full attention, Sean felt pretty certain she wouldn't be slinging her tour binder at him.

"If you can bear with me a bit longer, I promise I'll make this stop worth your while. Last month, someone very stubborn was dead set against dating anyone. Too much trouble, too busy, the usual excuses. Then he met someone who pulled him away from his fishing hole, so to speak. You don't mind a few fishing references, do you? This is Sturgeon Widows Tours, after all."

A lady behind Darcy leaned forward and whispered something to her he couldn't hear. Then she reached over the seat, patting Darcy on the shoulder.

"Anyway, this person helped him see that love isn't as elusive as a full-bellied muskie, even though at the time he preferred his dog for company, and any sound other than his fly line snapping over Sage Creek annoyed the hell out of him."

The knowing smiles began to appear, and eyes darted between him and Darcy. The woman nearest him clutched the arm of her friend.

Sean dared to look at Darcy for a second and that was enough for him to choke on what he would say next. He swallowed a few times and grinned at her as she clutched the top of the seat in front of her, those chestnut eyes wide enough he could see them glistening even from halfway across the bus.

"So while this spot might not yet be an official stop on our tour, it's the most significant to me because—"

He paused because she stood up again and came forward. Darcy looked up at him, her features growing soft, the corners of her mouth twitching with a smile.

"Didn't I tell you to sit down, Conti? You're messing up my—what'd you call it on that first day? My *schtick?*"

"There's nothing wrong with your *schtick,*" she said, her voice low.

He kissed her then, even with a bus full of strangers for an audience, something he never would have *ever* considered before with anyone, but he could no longer stand not to because they were like two magnets finally within range of each other. His arms encircled her, pulling her against him, twisting her around to his other side so he could shield them from their guests. Her breath caught as their lips parted. She rested her head on his shoulder, and her hand slid up his chest, past his neck, threading itself through his hair, pulling him farther into her kiss. Sean didn't want it to end, couldn't bring himself to let her go, her soft lips awakening his hunger for more as always, but there was a clearing of several throats, some snickering, and someone whispered, "I think they forgot about us."

When they drew apart, Darcy used his lapel to dry the moist spot at the corner of her eye. She laughed, glancing over his shoulder at their guests. "I think they're waiting for you to finish what you were saying."

"I'm not finished with *you* yet."

"Oh?"

Sean held her face in his hands. She thought another kiss was imminent, but then he drew back slightly to study her. His earnest expression dulled the buzz filling Darcy's head, yet she strained to hear him when he said something under his breath.

"I didn't hear you."

Sean glanced sideways, suddenly self-conscious of the audience, then he looked back at her. "I said I love you," he whispered.

Darcy's mind raced. A scrambled assortment of replies tumbled around in her head, words that didn't do justice to how she felt. They sat at the back of her throat, too big and important to be spoken lightly. She swallowed, her mouth suddenly dry.

"Really?" she croaked, then looked down at her feet, shaking her head. That wasn't what she meant.

He laughed. "Is it so hard to believe? I know I've been impossible—"

She took a deep breath, then another and looked up at

him. "I love you too," she said. The words came fast, too fast, but by the look on his face, the grin that played on his lips, they were the right words.

Sean looked at her a moment longer; he stood close enough that she could see the creases on his lips. Then he faced the bus, loosening his hold on Darcy. "Sorry for the slight deviation to plans. I'm going to finish by saying this spot is important to me because I've been hooked. Again, I can't help the fishing puns."

"She wouldn't dare toss you back!" someone shouted. "You're a keeper!"

A knock on the door interrupted everyone's laughter. It was Ingrid.

Sean opened the door so she could step onto the bus. "Sorry. Running a bit behind schedule."

Ingrid looked at the bus full of passengers. "Did you tell them I'm on the tour itinerary because I make the best chocolate cream pies in the upper Midwest?" she said. "Your mother's inside wondering what's been taking so long."

Sean huffed. "Those pies were bribery because you knew what I had planned. You and my mother aren't as slick as you think."

"I thought Emily wasn't feeling well?" Darcy asked.

Sean chuckled. "You don't know my mother very well."

The afternoon tour had started with Sean's announcement of the plans for Blueberry Point Lodge, and Ingrid's luscious cream pie and coffee for the guests in the house's atrium. It ended three hours later with hugs and handshakes for Sean and Darcy on the patio at Sturgeon Widows Tours. The afternoon sun dipped behind the trees, cooling the air considerably. Yet despite the dropping temperature, the women lingered in the leaf-littered courtyard.

"That was the most romantic gesture I've seen in a long time," said a woman as Darcy thanked her and said goodbye. She was petite, and wore a silver shell pinned on her jacket lapel. The woman pointed her finger in Sean's direction. "The world needs more of that."

Still somewhat stunned by Sean's revelation, Darcy smiled. "I agree, but I don't think that'll be on the itinerary every time. That caught me completely by surprise."

The woman leaned in close, whispering, "A man who professes his feelings in public like that, especially one as private as your guy, is someone who has your back for life."

Darcy took a step back, surprised by the personal nature of the woman's words.

"Oh, I don't mean to embarrass you, dear. Simply calling it as I see it. He reminds me a lot of my late husband. It's refreshing."

"Thank you," Darcy said.

A quick glance toward Sean found him at the center of attention in the middle of five women. He gestured toward Clem and said something, causing heads to tilt back in laughter. She loved that he was so affable with their guests, but with her, he acted as if she were the whole world. She noticed that while they had been shuttling guests all afternoon. Every time Sean looked at her, it seemed he struggled to look away, as if the sight of her was life-sustaining.

How wrong she had been this past week.

Chapter Twenty

❦

Word got around Hendricks in a hurry that Darcy and Sean were suddenly inseparable after their brief "misunderstanding," thanks in part to the conspiratorial shenanigans of Emily and Ingrid, though the two women emphatically denied any involvement. In fact, the different versions of the truth amused Darcy as she spent the next week dispelling rumors that she and Sean were either engaged, already married after eloping and making a trip to Kakabeka Falls in less than twenty-four hours, or moving out of state because of her new job as the lead researcher of a 17th-century shipwreck somewhere in the Caribbean.

"Where did that one come from?" Sean asked her on a Sunday morning during the first week of November. He sat with Darcy in the upstairs foyer of Blueberry Point Lodge, enjoying the lake view. It was a gloriously frosty morning.

Ice crystals blanketed the landscape like a winter wedding gown.

"You're asking me how small-town gossip escalates? I thought you were more of the expert in that department?" She rewrapped her oversized flannel scarf around her shoulders to ward off the chill. As much as she loved sitting before the floor-to-ceiling multipaned window, it was a drafty spot when the weather turned cold.

Sean grimaced. "Some rumors are enigmas."

"No kidding. Never mind that we've only known each other for—what?—a little over two months?"

He looked toward the ceiling, thinking. "Fifty-nine days."

Darcy stared at him, fighting a grin. He was full of surprises.

The clattering of dishes from the lower level sounded as if Ingrid and Henry were finished cleaning up after breakfast. Then she and Sean would help the older couple with packing. She sipped her coffee, and finished off the last bite of the cinnamon roll that Debi had tucked in the box of donuts Darcy picked up the day before at the shop.

"This was sweet of Debi." Darcy licked the stickiness from her fingers. The roll was easily the best she'd ever eaten. "Does she give away rolls often?"

"It might have something to do with you being a loyal customer."

Darcy glanced at him, wondering if he'd elaborate.

"Never mind. Did I tell you that Matt apologized, by the way?"

"What for?"

"There was no ruptured gas line the morning he drove

the tour. He covered for me during my appointment at the bank. Preliminary financial stuff."

"I'll have to thank him for lying." She took a sip from her mug and gazed out at the water, its surface undulating like liquid diamonds. "So when did you actually decide to buy this place?"

"As soon as Ingrid told my mom she needed to sell. Aidan showing up just happened to speed the process is all."

Darcy reached out and took his hand. "I actually feel sorry for the guy." When the corners of Sean's mouth dipped, she squeezed him. "But only a little bit. He put a lot of work into his plans. No wonder he wasn't returning my calls during that last week."

"Ha! His plans would have completely ruined this place." Sean looked at their interlocking fingers. "I want to apologize for something too."

Darcy looked at him. "What's that?"

"I misread you. I shouldn't have compared you to something—to Paige—and shut you out."

She twisted in her seat so she could see him fully. "I love this place, this town. I told you that day on the beach. I've found my home here."

Sean leaned forward and kissed her, a moist, lingering one that left her feeling buoyant.

"Maybe I was too afraid to believe it." He drew back and studied her while he took her hand. "I'm trying to take it a day at a time. Wondering about the future at this point just complicates things."

Darcy squeezed his hand. "There's nothing wrong with

looking ahead. Besides, we're way past all of the misread signals. I'd like to think we know each other better by now."

He kissed her again, a soft, fleeting touch on her lips, which left the spot tingling. Then he stood to take in the view from the window. "So. What are your plans for the house other than hosting guests for overnight stays?"

"You tell me. Buying it was your idea. You must have something in mind." His question raised a larger question though. Exactly what role would she play at Sturgeon Widows Tours? She loved that he asked her for advice, but her duties in his family's company weren't up to her.

"The only thing I'm personally going to see to is getting a locked gate installed on the path to our private beach."

Darcy raised her eyebrows. "I like that idea."

"And what do you think about building a few more cottages on the property?"

"You should probably talk to your family about that. I'm only your employee, after all."

He turned around and his eyes bore into her. "You're much more than that, Conti."

She barely managed a smile because Sean's expression held captive any words she could put together in a coherent sentence.

"The only disadvantage to owning this place is our business will have to operate out of two separate buildings for a while. The house needs some work."

Darcy stretched her legs out to rest her feet on the round table before her. "I'd really like to keep the events here intimate. That's part of the house's charm, the size of the rooms. Aidan's plans for demolishing walls gave me headaches for days."

"I agree. I'll keep Matt busy enough with building the cabins. I don't think he'd like the idea of opening up rooms in this place either."

"I'm so happy for you," Darcy said, standing. She walked into his arms when he came toward her. She kissed him, then nestled her face into the heady warmth of his neck. "I love that this place is in your family again. I bet the house is happy too."

His chuckle vibrated through his body into hers. "It's even happier that you're sticking around."

When Sean took her cup downstairs to refill it, her gaze returned to the water. A light-headed joy filled her then, touching every part of her, yet finding the space too constrictive, seemed to push against the confines of her body, beating to be released, wanting to take flight. If the lake were a testament to how she felt at the moment, its surface like blue glass radiating the sun's brilliance, she might liken it to everything she knew was right in her life. What could she call that feeling other than what it was?

It was something real, all right. Something real and true, like the water.

Acknowledgments

To the following people, I owe something more than a few words of thanks in the back of a book, but this will have to do for now:

—To the Craddock family for your friendship and hospitality. Thanks to you, writing with the Big Lake as a backdrop brought this story to life and makes me wish for a cabin of our own.

—To Lia London-Gubelin, Rachel John, and Maggie Zapp for stepping forward as trusted, competent readers.

— Deep gratitude to Hollie Westring for weeding out the extraneous stuff with her careful eye. With each pass, it became a better, tighter story.

—To Jenny Zemanek for her gorgeous cover design skills, which perfectly captured Hendricks as I envisioned it.

—And lastly, to my family for their love and continuous support. Living a writerly life would not be possible without you.

Love Like Fire

COMING NOVEMBER 2018

❧❀❧

If there was one thing Bethany Marconi was good at—
no, *excelled* at—it was matchmaking. Never mind the
number of blind dates which had gone up in flames.
Bethany didn't count them since they were few and far
between, and admittedly, she wasn't *that* good. What
mattered were the relationships that *had* worked out. Those
which rode out the pitfalls after the honeymoon months
wore off and before the engagement announcement. She
counted four weddings to date, the result of her introducing
the lovebirds at the onset. That was why she was out the
door in five minutes when her best friend, Darcy Conti,
called in dire need of a shoulder to cry on. Darcy and Sean
Stetman would be the fifth wedding. Someday. As soon as
Stetman got his act together and proposed.

"We just had our first fight," Darcy had said earlier. "I
need to talk. I'm going crazy."

Bethany grabbed her wallet and keys with one hand

while she balanced the phone between her cheek and shoulder. "Meet you at Debi's in ten minutes. Scone and coffee is on me."

Bethany wheeled into the first parking space in front of Debi's Donuts, a diminutive place with pink siding and gingerbread trim. Beyond the building, Lake Superior reflected the clear January sky, a liquid sheet of cerulean glass. The colors were a beautiful contrast, and when Bethany stepped out of her car, she took a moment to breathe deeply and revel in the scenery.

She'd console and listen. She'd let Darcy talk for what, five minutes, maybe? Then and only then would she open her mouth. Improving her listening skills was her New Year's resolution. She'd been doing fairly well, given that she'd been at it a solid week. It was part of her living mindfully project, and admittedly, it was *hard*.

Darcy's Jeep pulled in behind her. Even through the windshield, Bethany could tell Darcy was upset. Her raven curls, usually loose around her shoulders, were tamed in a headband, which wouldn't be a telltale sign of her mood necessarily, but with her hair swept off her face, the angry slashes of her eyebrows were on full display.

Bethany opened Darcy's car door and stood aside as her friend struggled to get out of the driver's seat without unfastening her belt. Frustrated, Darcy unhooked the belt, but then her bag handle wrapped around the shift lever and pulled her back onto the seat.

Darcy groaned and pounded the steering wheel, the horn emitting an abrupt honk that startled two ravens resting on the pitched roof of the donut shop. She yanked the bag out of the car and slammed the door. "If one more thing doesn't go right today, I'm seriously going to empty my bank account and run away."

"I don't think I've ever seen you quite so…animated."

Darcy shook her head, slinging her bag over one shoulder. "This is nothing. You should have seen me after I got off the phone with Sean."

Bethany opened the door for Darcy, and the two walked into the euphoria of sweetness. Debi's place brought about an instant calm, though Bethany wondered if anything could soothe Darcy at the moment. As naturally wired as her friend was, Bethany had never known Darcy to act this flustered.

She opened her wallet and pointed to the window seat. "Go sit down. The usual?"

Darcy sighed. "Yes, please, though no coffee. That would just fuel my ranting."

"Maybe you need to rant. Better to me than to Sean."

A few minutes later, Bethany brought the warm scones cradled in their napkins to where Darcy waited, drumming her fingers on the tabletop.

Bethany slid into the vinyl booth. "Okay. Spill it."

Darcy's shoulders slumped as she relaxed against the back of the booth. She stuck a stirrer into her coffee mug. "Sean has been under a lot of stress—making repairs at the lodge and driving the tours. He doesn't have much downtime."

"Yes, you've mentioned that."

Darcy looked out the window toward the water. "Well, I mentioned that I was going to Marquette for a long weekend to see Mom. I'm taking Friday off since we don't have a tour booked," she said, glancing at Bethany before she continued stirring her coffee absentmindedly.

"Go on." Bethany guessed where this was heading, wanted to ask if she was right, but her silent pledge was still only seconds old. *Keep it zipped.*

"I casually asked if he wanted to come with, you know, so he wouldn't feel left out of my plans. And he totally snapped." Darcy threw up her hands. "I was only thinking of him, yet he accused me of suggesting he can just drop everything and take off."

Bethany nodded knowingly. Yes, she knew exactly the trigger in that scenario. Old flames die hard.

"The Ghost of Paige." So much for listening.

Darcy nodded. "You got it. He didn't mention her by name, but I did, and that was my mistake. But being compared to her drives me crazy. Completely nuts! Or the *thought* of the comparison, that is."

Bethany brushed the crumbs off her pants that had fallen into her lap. "What did you say exactly?"

Darcy gritted her teeth. "You know my problem with filtering words, right?"

"Just tell me. Maybe it's not as bad as you think."

She groaned. "I said if he's still stuck on what happened in the past, maybe he's not ready for a future with me."

"Harsh but true."

Darcy shrank farther into the booth. "That's not all."

"Uh-oh."

"Yeah." Darcy swirled the stir stick a few more times. "I said that I didn't want him to go after all because he clearly loves his job more than me." She looked at Bethany. "That's along the same lines of what Paige said to him before he broke up with her."

It was Bethany's turn to cringe. "Yikes. He told you that?"

"Yes."

"And how did you guys end the conversation?"

"I hung up on him."

Bethany grabbed the stick out of Darcy's cup, ending the maddening repetition of stick stirring. "Well, you'll just have to call him back and apologize."

"I knew you'd say that."

"What other solution is there? You screwed up. It won't get better by ignoring it."

"I know. That's what mature couples do, right? Apologize?"

Bethany felt like saying she didn't really know from personal experience, but yes, that usually happened in every romance novel she read. Whoever screws up says as many sorries as necessary if the couple has any chance of staying together. Apart from her romantic literary expertise, Bethany never got to the point in a relationship to apologize. The first fight was typically the last fight, then she'd cut her new ex-boyfriend loose so he could lick his wounds and wonder what natural disaster occurred to upend his love life so completely. Romantic bliss and Bethany were not synonymous.

"Wh-what if he's not okay with me apologizing?" Darcy's eyebrows dipped as she looked away. The firm set of her mouth told Bethany that her friend was considering the worst-case scenario.

"Darcy, don't be ridiculous. Sean loves you."

Darcy chewed on her lip, shaking her head slightly.

"What, you doubt that? C'mon, seriously? He'd be the ground you walk on if it were physically possible. He worships you."

"I know he does." Darcy sighed. "He's been working so hard, too, and I had to use that against him. I'm rotten."

"We all are on occasion."

"You never have problems like this. What's your secret?"

"When was the last time I dated someone longer than a couple months?"

Darcy looked at her blankly.

Bethany held her finger up. "That's my secret."

They laughed together, and Bethany could tell the joke eased some of Darcy's tension, because she finally took a bite of her scone.

"Why is that, Bethany? Seriously. You're never lacking for dates. A lot of them are nice guys, too, from what I can tell."

It was Bethany's turn to look inward, something she was as good at as keeping boyfriends. If she thought deep enough, the reasons turned toward her career-obsessed parents, and Gran, who essentially raised her, and those were thoughts for another day.

"I just don't like to be tied down, I guess. Too much to do without lovey-dovey stuff to tend to."

Darcy smiled. "You're funny." Darcy's look lingered on Bethany. "I like your hair, by the way. What'd you do to it?"

Bethany shrugged and fluffed one side. "Cropped it a

little shorter. Got it lightened. I'm still not used to having nothing below my shoulders."

"I love it. It suits you."

"Thanks. I think winter was the wrong time to go shorter though. I swear my neck has frostbite."

Darcy laughed. "You'll get used to it." After a moment, the smile faded from Darcy's face. "There's something else that has been kind of bothering me too."

"What's that?"

"Funny you brought up the Ghost of Paige, because she's not going to be just a memory soon." Darcy nodded when Bethany's mouth popped open. "Yeah, she's coming to town."

"What for?" Bethany's voice squeaked with incredulity.

"She was assigned a photo feature of the North Shore for *Travel America* magazine. Since we expanded with the lodge, she'll be doing a side article on Sturgeon Widows Tours."

"Did she call you?"

"She called the company, and Sean happened to answer. He mentioned her calling but didn't want to say much more about it. I think he's mad more than anything—mad that he'll have to put up with her for a few days."

"You could be the contact person for her. Wouldn't that be a hoot?"

Darcy laughed. "Don't think I didn't consider it."

Bethany sipped her coffee. "Well, let me know if you need me. First fight aside, there's nothing that would make me happier than a happily ever after for you two. And anything—or anyone—who gets in the way... Well, watch out."

"I know. Thanks for listening," Darcy said. She patted the top of Bethany's hand. "That reminds me. Tickets go on sale this week for the Red Hot Gala. It's the weekend before Valentine's Day. Consider this a call to action to find a date."

Bethany rubbed her hands together. "I'll have to think about the timing carefully. If I find someone too soon, there's the chance he won't be in the picture come February."

"True. And you won't want to miss our inaugural gala at Blueberry Point Lodge. It's going to be magical."

"With you in charge, I don't doubt that."

Darcy drained her mug. "I should get to work. Hopefully I can catch Sean without his mother or Melina there." She slid out of the booth and hugged Bethany. "Thanks again. You're always the voice of reason."

Bethany laughed. "I think you're exaggerating. I'm just a good listener. But thanks."

Darcy left with a bounce in her step, and Bethany smiled to herself while she wiped the table free of crumbs and finished the last swallow of coffee. It had taken forever to get those two together, even though Bethany knew they'd be perfect for each other. They'd only been dating four months, a time when those little insecurities started to creep in and upend everything. But she wouldn't know that from personal experience. No way. And she wouldn't find out any time soon either if it was up to her.

About the Author

D.E. Malone is the author of the *Hearts in Hendricks* contemporary romance series which debuts in Summer 2018 with her first title, LOVE LIKE WATER. She has also written two middle-grade novels, BINGO SUMMER and THE UPSIDE OF DOWN, as Dawn Malone, as well as essays, short stories, and articles for the CHICKEN SOUP FOR THE SOUL series, *Highlights for Children*, the *Wisconsin State Journal*, and other newspapers and magazines. When she's not writing, she can be found reading, biking, and hiking if someone else carries her backpack. She lives in central Illinois.

If you enjoyed reading LOVE LIKE WATER, please consider leaving a review at www.amazon.com or www.goodreads.com. You'll find the latest book news and release dates by signing up for my newsletter on my blog, Here's the Story, http://dawnmalone.blogspot.com. I can also be found on Facebook, Instagram, Pinterest, and Twitter @dmalonebooks.